HOARDED SECRETS

NIGHTWOOD CLAN SERIES, BOOK 6

HARPER DAKOTA

Cover Design by: Jay Aheer

Editing by: Lori Parks

Warning:

This book contains mature themes and is intended to be read by ages 18+. Contains sex, some curse words, paranormal and magical themes, fated mates, and some secondary characters are a male/male couple. The death of a sibling and parents are mentioned, but occurred in the past and is not detailed. Main character is kidnapped and held without food, mild violence.

Trademark Acknowledgements:

The author acknowledges the following trademarks and trademark status of these items mentioned in the book, including:

Library Lion by Michelle Knudsen

Post-it

Ticket to Ride

Sorry

Monopoly

To my family. Thank you. I love you all bunches.

To all those amazing people who have helped me along the way, including my husband, my beta readers, my proofreader, cover designer, and formatter. You guys are amazing. Thank you.

HOARDED SECRETS

Marge is content being the librarian and the Guardian of the paranormal library in the small town of Rockfort. As an only child whose mother left at an early age, Marge has been on her own for a long time. When the Nightwood Clan starts to embrace her into their family, she's a little shocked. She certainly never thought Fate would send her a mate of her own.

Duncan came to Rockfort to avenge his sister. Now a year later, he's back. He has no idea why he's here, just that he felt drawn to return. It's been a long time since he's had a home, but the town and the Clan feel like family to him. When trouble hits the town, he wants to help. He just never thought it would include saving the mate he's never met.

Despite finding a family and each other, Duncan and Marge have other issues to fight. It seems like there's corruption within the paranormal government, corruption that will affect their new family.

Will the family be able to save themselves? Or will they lose one of their own?

PRE-NOTE FROM THE AUTHOR

Thank you for choosing my book to read! I hope you enjoy it.

If this is your first time reading one of my books, or it has been a while in between reads, here are some helpful things so you don't feel lost.

There is a character list in the back of the book.

Mates and members of the Clan can speak telepathically to each other. This type of communication is indicated with a single apostrophe and the words are in italic.
Example: *'I can't wait to see you,'* Marge said.

Text messages are indicated with a name in capital letters and are in bold with a colon.
Example:
MARGE: I'll be there soon.
DUNCAN: Drive safely.

Nightwood Clan members and their respective mates:
Rolf (Rolfston) - Shaye

Sam - Tess
Doc (Albert) – Emma
Ian - Berkley
Gawain - Merri (Meredith)
Duncan - Marge

PROLOGUE

Merri pulled on the library door, but it was still locked. That was strange. On days like this, when they were going to be working before it was officially open, they had started the tradition of eating breakfast together. Today was Merri's day to bring in goodies. Marge normally had the back door unlocked already and would be waiting in their little break room slash office. Balancing the cups of tea in one hand, Merri pulled out her keys and opened the heavy wood door.

"Marge? I brought tea and some muffins for breakfast. Are we still working on cataloguing the new items in the back room this morning?" Merri called out as she walked in.

The lights were still out, no sounds of movement or Marge calling back. Merri stopped, setting the drink carrier and bag of food down on the entrance table. Pulling out her phone, she dialed Marge. In the depths of the library, she could hear the phone ringing, no sign of Marge answering.

'Guys, I think I need help at the library. All the lights are off, the doors were locked when I got here, and Marge's phone is ringing somewhere inside but she's not answering,' she said over the Clan link.

'I'll be right there. Merri, are you in the front or the back?' Ian asked.

'Back door to the office,' she replied.

Seconds later, she heard a sound outside.

"Merri, it's me," Ian said through the door.

"I forgot just how fast you are," Merri said with a stressed laugh as she opened the door. "This isn't like Marge, and I have a bad feeling."

"Never hesitate to call us if something feels wrong. Berkley was going to get Gage to meet us. Let's stay put until they get here. Rolf and Gawain were at the museum, they're on the way too."

'Merri, Emma, Shaye, Doc, and I are at the clinic. We're in with patients right now, but if you need us, we can ask Sherri to reschedule the non-emergency appointments for today,' Tess offered.

'Ian's here and Rolf and Gawain are on their way. Berkley went to get Gage, so I should have enough people here. It's eerie, something is off. Stay with your patients. If anything changes, I'll let you know,' Merri replied.

The door flew open, and Gawain rushed inside.

"Are you okay?" he asked worriedly.

Merri nodded, walking into her mate's arms for a hug. Gage followed him inside, squeezing around them.

"Okay, tell me what's going on. Berkley just told me to get down here. He was locking up the store and will be right down, Rolf's standing outside guarding the door," Gage said, his hand on his gun belt.

"This sounds silly," Merri replied. "When I got here, the doors were locked. I know it's before opening, but we were going to catalogue some new items in the back room before we officially opened. We eat breakfast together on early days and she normally is waiting in here with the door unlocked. I walked in, called out for Marge, and didn't get a response. All the lights were off. I called her phone; I can hear it ringing in the library but there's no answer."

"I got here soon after she called out over the Clan link," Ian added. "I don't sense anyone else in here, and Marge's cat is hard to miss. I do smell something though," he said, looking pointedly at Gage, whose eyes widened slightly when he realized that Ian meant he could smell blood.

The door opened again, and Berkley walked in with Rolf. "What's—" he started. He stopped and immediately started a protection spell.

"What is it?" Rolf asked. He knew that look on Berkley's face, and it wasn't good.

"There was magic thrown around here recently. Not good magic. Everyone stay close to Gage or me until we make sure it's safe. Merri, can you flip on the lights?" Berkley asked.

Gage moved with Merri toward the master light switch panel. Opening the door to the main room, she flipped the lights on and gasped. The library was trashed. There were books on the floor, the lamp on the help desk hanging by its cord, the shade shattered. Merri rushed to the desk, but Gage grabbed her before she got there.

"Just a minute, Merri. Let me go first," he said gently.

She waited, trying to peer over the desk to see what he was looking at.

"Ian, can you come here?" Gage asked.

Merri watched as Ian walked around to the backside of the desk, then seemed to follow a trail. He walked all the way to the paranormal room's door. He jiggled the handle, but it was locked. Pressing an ear to the door, he came back to the desk and shook his head.

"I don't think anyone is in there," he said.

"What did you find?" Merri questioned. "What happened?"

Gage motioned for her to come around. The computer screen was cracked, blood drying on the desk. She saw a few drops on the ground leading away from the door. That must have been what Ian was following.

"Whose is that?" Merri asked, desperately hoping that it wasn't Marge's.

"It smells like Marge and someone else," Ian said quietly. "I don't recognize the other scent."

"There's something here that's familiar," Gage said, his nostrils flaring as he took a deep breath. "I'm going to need to call Marco in. He's a better tracker than I am."

Merri looked around, hoping to find any sign of Marge. Maybe she was hiding, Merri thought desperately. Her eyes caught on something glittering under the desk. Dropping to her knees, she crawled under the desk to get the object barely visible underneath the drawers. All her hope vanished, her heart dropping and a sob escaping as she saw Marge's keys. She never would have left them here unprotected.

'Merri? What happened?' Shaye asked. *'Are you hurt?'*

Merri shook her head, knowing Shaye couldn't see her. She opened the Clan link once more, even though half of them were here, it would be easier to tell the rest of them at once.

'Marge is gone. She's been taken.'

Berkley looked over sharply. "Why do you say that? She could just be hiding from whoever broke in."

"Marge would never leave her keys lying around. Those are the library keys, and one is to the paranormal room. She wouldn't leave them unprotected. If she lost them, then something huge was happening. If she tossed them there, she was trying to hide them in a hurry."

"Has anyone strange been coming into the library? Anything new going on?" Gage asked.

"We had a shipment of books come in. I'm not entirely sure from where, but they were older paranormal books. We didn't really examine them yet, but we did flip through a few. Based on the information in the books when we glanced through one, they were written by paranormals. There were things in there that wouldn't be known to a human. There was also a protective spell over the box. I scanned it before we opened it to make sure it wasn't dangerous, but it dissipated as soon as Marge touched it. It had been addressed to her," Merri replied, clenching the keys tight.

"Were you going to work on those today?" Gage asked. He had a bad feeling that Marge's disappearance had something to do with the shipment.

"We were. We had locked them in the back room as soon as they arrived. Until we got them sorted and added magical protections, if needed, we weren't opening the back room. Marge talked about making a storage area in the back room for incidents like this, but right now there is nowhere else to put them here that would be as safe," Merri replied.

"Can you tell if someone came into the library late last night?" Rolf asked. "Do you have security cameras?"

"I think we do on the doors, but I'm not entirely sure how to access those," Merri admitted. "I hadn't been trained on that yet. I could look to see if someone requested access to a book in the back though."

"If you closed the area, why would they submit a request?" Gawain asked.

"We didn't put a sign up. Most of our human patrons assume it's just storage or stairs to the basement and we didn't want to draw attention to it. If they're human, they might not know a book they were requesting was a paranormal book. If they were paranormal, we were going to tell them it would take a couple of days to get whatever they requested ready for them, and we would call and let them know when to come back in."

Merri looked at the computer screen. There was no way she could use that; the screen was completely smashed. She grabbed her key and opened one of the drawers to grab out the tablet. It would take her a minute to log on and get into the paranormal form database.

"Would someone hae been able to get in the back wi' Marge's keys?" Ian asked. "Could that be why she hid them?" If they were that important, he couldn't see her losing them. He would bet she deliberately tossed them. The blood trail to the back room certainly made it look like they had tried to force Marge to open the door.

Merri shook her head. "Marge always had them. She's the Guardian of the library. There are wards on the back room that would keep someone out, even if they had the key, if they were ill-intentioned or had been banned from another library." The tablet vibrated in her hands, alerting her that her log-in had gone through. "It looks like someone was trying to get access to the back room. The last entry is a denial."

Merri placed the tablet on the counter so the rest of her family could see. "I don't recognize the name, but the system logs a person's essence, not whatever name they're using. See how this area is red? That means that the person has been banned from here or another paranormal library. If it was orange, they would be human and not allowed to enter. Green would be good to go, either as a paranormal or a human mated to a paranormal."

"I need to get Marco in here," Gage said, pulling out his phone. "It's not a name I recognize either, but there's something about the scent that is familiar and it's not Marge's."

"Hey. I need you in town. Something happened at the library. Keep it quiet," Gage said before hanging up.

There was a slight disturbance in the air and Marco was suddenly standing there. He took a deep breath before asking, "What the fuck happened?"

Gage ran him through what they knew. "I recognize one of the other scents, but I can't place it. Can you?"

Marco stepped closer to the blood on the desk, closing his eyes to draw a long deep breath. Merri could sense his shifter side coming closer to the surface, the air suddenly thicker and more tense. Her body was telling her to run away screaming, even though she knew it was Marco, someone who had helped them in the past. She had no idea what his beast side was, but it had to be an extremely powerful predator. She noticed Berkley had his hands ready to cast a protection spell and Gawain was gripping her arm. Rolf had moved himself to stand between her and Marco, Ian right behind her. While they all thought of Marco in friendly terms, they had never experienced this level of power being emanated from him before and it must have riled up all of them.

"Son of a bitch," he suddenly yelled.

"What?" Gage asked him impatiently.

"There's an underlying scent that I know, but something's stopping me from recognizing it. I think they're using a blocker of some kind. I know I've smelled this before, multiple times in fact. Most recently the last time in the woods," Marco said, frustration in his voice.

Merri breathed a lot more freely as his power was suddenly sucked back in, leaving him as they would normally sense him.

"We've got a problem," Marco said, looking at everyone.

1

Marge began shutting off the lights in the paranormal room before she shut the door, making sure it was locked. She was excited to go through the collection tomorrow with Merri. She wasn't sure where the books had come from, but she would put out a few feelers to see if an old mentor or acquaintance had sent them to her. For now though, they were safe. Merri would come back a couple of hours before opening. If they weren't done before the first patrons arrived, one of them could always work in the back while the other manned the front desk. Or they could come in early the next day. She was excited. It had been a long time since she had new materials in the paranormal room.

Her stomach rumbled, letting her know that it didn't appreciate her skipping lunch. The library had been extremely busy today, and the minutes she had of free time were spent bringing the box to the back room and flipping through a few of the materials. Now she couldn't think of something easy she had in the fridge for dinner. Maybe a can of soup would take the edge off before she made a more filling dinner. Just ten more minutes and she could lock the front doors. Marge walked around, picking up a few stray books, shaking her head when she saw the stuffed lion in the children's area posed with the book *The Library Lion*. Merri must have set that up before she left. She was so glad Merri decided to work at the library. Marge hadn't realized just how lonely she had become. The whole Nightwood Clan had welcomed her in when she had shown up for dinner and a run through the woods. Merri had been right in that they simply accepted her for who she was, and seemed to know when she became overwhelmed and needed a bit of space. She still wasn't comfortable enough to go over every week for their family Sunday dinners, although she had an open invitation. She had heard Gage received one as well.

Hearing the chime for the front door, she called out, "I'll be there in a moment," before putting the books on one of the little tables. She would help this last person and then close up. She could finish the books once the doors were locked.

Her cat hissed inside her head, agitated over something. Marge took a deep breath, trying to scent what the issue might be. There were several smells, but they were confusing. She knew she was smelling something, but she couldn't place what it was. She could almost feel the hair on her arms stand up; this wasn't a natural occurrence, whoever came in was using a spell or scent blocker. She wanted to call someone, but she had left her cell phone up at the desk, locked in the drawer. It was normally quiet in town, and it was her habit to put her phone away; it wasn't like she had a lot of people calling. Gage and Merri, or sometimes the other Nightwood Clan members, would stop in since they were so close. If she could reach it, she could call Gage or even Merri for backup. Merri could send some of the guys over. Marge made sure her keys were hidden in her pocket and wouldn't rattle.

Walking past the row of books, she could see four men standing at the front desk. She still couldn't scent what they were, either paranormal or human, which only confirmed that they were using a blocker. Neither one was good, although she could probably hold her own in a fight against a few humans as long as they didn't have weapons.

"We're closing in a few minutes," she said as she walked to the desk. "I can see if I can help you quickly, or if it's a longer search, I'll have to help you tomorrow." She had to work hard at keeping her heartbeat steady when she noticed two more men in the shadows by the door. She couldn't make out their features.

"We're looking for a book," one of the men said. His voice was gruff, something not ringing quite true. She noticed the men by the desk all had a pendant on. So, they were using a blocking spell. Shit. She didn't want to draw attention to her keys in case they were trying to get access to the back room, so she wasn't going to be able to grab her cell phone to call anyone. Maybe she could use the library phone, play it off like she was checking with someone else about what they needed.

"Let me log back on and I can look that up for you," she replied. "Alright, what's the name of the book?"

"*Creatures of the Myth*. It would have been published a hundred years ago or more."

"Give me a second to see what I can find." Marge knew darn well that book was in the paranormal room. Even without the form, her cat instincts were telling her these guys were no good. She hummed and acted like she was searching even longer. Her screen clearly showed '*archives, back,*' which just confirmed it was in the back room. "It looks like it's in an archived area. I'll need you to fill out a form and it will be ready in a day or so. Make sure to leave your phone number so I can let you know when it's ready." Marge bent down to grab the form, sliding her keys out of her pocket, and dropping them down behind the desk drawers. She used her foot to scoot them out of sight. If they simply left, she'd get them back, but if they tried force her to open the door, at least they wouldn't have access to her keys. It wasn't the best hiding spot, but Merri would eventually find them if something happened to her. She watched as the speaker of the group filled out the paperwork, a couple of his friends pointing to something on the form. At least all of them would be imprinted into the system. The man brought the form over to one of the men in the shadows. This guy filled in something. As soon as it was brought over, she pretended to look it over, noticing the phone number was in a different handwriting. To no one's surprise the computer screen showed a red bar, indicating at least one of them had been banned from another paranormal library. It also flashed an orange bar, indicating one of them was human and not a paranormal mate.

The man in the shadows took a step closer. "Have you had any new releases or deliveries?"

Marge swallowed. They had to be after the mystery shipment of books that had just arrived. "We get donations occasionally, and new releases are displayed on that table right where you walked in," she replied, trying to stay calm. Her pulse jumped as one of the men came around the backside of the desk, another standing at either side, essentially trapping her in.

She reached out, grabbing the library's phone. "I can call and ask the other employee if there are any new releases that aren't out on display yet. She's in charge of the fiction section." She knew she would need to give a logical reason for calling, but she didn't want throw Merri under their suspicion either. These weren't fiction books, so they shouldn't go looking for her. She got three numbers dialed before a hand grabbed her wrist, squeezing hard enough that she dropped the phone. Looking up, it was the man in the shadows.

"No," he said simply. "I know the database must have told you by now that at least one of us is banned. No phone calls for backup. Pat her down. Make sure she doesn't have a cell phone," he ordered. Two of the flunkies grabbed her other arm, while a third patted her down, grabbing her breasts as he went. When Gropey shook his head, the man in charge took hold of her arm, twisting it a bit behind her. "Now, you're going to open the restricted room and let us in. There's a book that we need that was delivered to your library."

"I haven't gone through all the books that were donated yet," Marge told them.

"I don't need you to go through the books. I'll find it. I need you to open the door." He twisted enough that it was starting to get really painful, her body moving with it to try to lessen the pressure.

Marge knew this wasn't going to end well. It didn't matter if she opened the door, the wards wouldn't let them pass. Her library had a few extra protections on it, which they must not know about. She didn't think they would simply leave when the wards wouldn't let them in. Marge briefly contemplated picking up her keys and seeing if she could make it into the room and shut them out, but quickly dismissed that thought. She was sure they would cause havoc amid the regular library, and she didn't want them to still be here when Merri or anyone else came in. No, the keys needed to stay hidden so they couldn't coerce someone who could get past the wards to get what they wanted. She would die before she let the integrity of the library and its books be compromised.

"I am the Guardian of the Library," she told him. "You will not get in that room," she stated firmly.

He laughed, causing his sycophants to join in. "I will get in that room one way or another. How quickly and how much pain you're in depends on you," he said almost congenially.

The air rushed from her lungs as one of the men behind her punched her in the side, the only thing holding her up was her stubbornness. Another punch landed on her other side, her ribs creaking. The guy had to be a paranormal; his hits were too strong to be human. A kick to the back of her knees dropped her to the ground, a hand grabbing her hair to slam her head against the countertop edge. The coppery scent and feeling of warmth told her that her skin had split. The idiots had let go of her arms when she fell. Drawing in a deep breath, she focused as much as she could, transforming her fingernails into the claws of her cat. It wasn't a trait most cat shifters had, but at least it gave her a bit of a weapon. Marge struck fast, driving her claws into the legs surrounding her, cutting the inner thigh of one of them. She didn't know if she got deep enough to hit the artery. Thrusting upward, she drove her hand into the stomach of the first man who had hit her, trying to disembowel him. Kicking back with one leg, she channeled her cat's strength to kick another halfway across the library. She could only hope that Gage could find them based on their scents when she made them bleed.

A kick to her stomach had her bending over, causing her to release the man before she could fully neutralize him. The position gave them the perfect opportunity to slam her head into the computer screen, hard enough that she heard the glass crack. Marge had a hard time making her eyes focus as she blinked.

"Bring her to the back," the man in charge ordered.

Someone grabbed her wrists, pulling them behind her, ensuring she couldn't attack them again. She leaned her head down, letting the blood drip on the floor. If they were going to kill her, she wanted to try to leave as many clues as possible for Gage. Luckily it looked like the men she had fought were also leaving blood drops.

Dragging her to the door, they tried to open it, throwing their bodies against the door and the surrounding wall when it wouldn't open.

"Go around the outside, break the windows."

Lifting her head, she could see a man minutes later outside the window. Clearly, he must have flown or scaled the wall, so probably a paranormal. He beat on the windows, even using a hammer he pulled from his pants. The windows held, the magic staying strong. The man in charge growled in frustration and wrenched one of her arms out in front of her. She gave a scream as she felt it dislocate at the shoulder. Slamming her hand on the doorknob, he tried to trick the magic into opening. Instead, the wards flexed, sensing her blood on the knob, a surge of magic pushing through the air, knocking them all back.

"We've been here too long. The wards clearly won't let us in. Take her with us. We'll find another way," he ordered.

Marge felt a pain in the back of her head. Everything went dark.

2

Marge woke, holding back a groan of pain. She panicked when she realized she couldn't move. She heard movement, the sounds of feet moving over dirt and rocks, a few twigs snapping. She forced herself to relax, to control her heartbeat and breathing. If she could pretend that she was still unconscious, then maybe she could figure out who some of them were and what they wanted. It would also give her time to try to find a way out of her bindings. She had no idea where they were, other than the fact that she could smell the damp earth, so they must be outside. Her ears picked up on birds chirping, squirrels running in the trees, but no sounds of traffic or other signs of being in or near a town. She hoped they didn't get too far away from Rockfort. She could see daylight through her closed eyes, so by now Merri would have discovered the library. Marge hated that Merri would have to see the mess, but at least someone would know she was gone. Merri would have called in the family and Gage, so they would be looking for her by now. Although the scent blockers the men were wearing would make that more difficult, her blood should help them scent track her. As long as they didn't throw a blocker on her. Well, if they didn't clean up her blood, her friends should still be able to track that.

"How hard did you hit her?" the guy in charge asked angrily. "If she's dead or brain damaged, I can't exactly ask her questions, now can I?"

"I didn't think I hit her that hard, b—" the voice cut off with a grunt as she heard the sound of flesh smacking.

"Boss, she should wake up soon," another voice chimed in.

"Get the water. Wake that cat up. I need answers," the boss demanded.

She heard feet shuffling away before she was hit with cold water right in the face. It had been angled to splash up her nose and she started coughing as she accidently inhaled some.

"It's about time. Pull her up," the boss ordered.

She held in a scream as she was yanked up by the hands bound behind her back. Sweat gathered on her forehead as she fought to keep from passing out. Her shoulder was still dislocated, the position and movement sending shards of pain through her. Opening her eyes, she saw her legs were cuffed together. She wondered if her hands were tied with rope or were in a metal type of cuff as well; she was having a hard time distinguishing sensation other than pain. She grunted as she was roughly shoved onto a log, fighting to maintain her balance as the hands holding her let go.

Her vision was still a little off and she worried what that meant. Her shifter healing should have taken care of the cut and a mild concussion by now. If she was still having issues, then either they drugged or spelled her with something, or the blows to the head had caused a lot of damage. She squinted, trying to make out the boss guy's features. He was tall, lean, dark hair. She couldn't make out his eye color from where she sat and with the sun shining behind him. The sun was going to be a problem, as it sent sharp stabs of pain through her head. She definitely had at least a really strong concussion.

"I need to know what books were recently brought into the library. I know there was a book about paranormals in there, mainly shifters. A register of sorts. I want that book and you can either send someone to get it, or you can get it and give it to me."

Marge could only image what he wanted with a register of shifters, but she knew it wouldn't be anything good. She thought about what Merri and Gage had told her was happening around the paranormal community and wondered if this guy was working with the corrupt members of the Convocation. Last she heard, Gage hadn't been sure if it was multiple groups working separately or if there was a figurehead controlling them all.

"Why would I help you? You attacked me, destroyed things in my library," Marge responded.

"It's in your own best interest. You're not leaving here until I have that book," he replied.

"How do you know it's in the library? I haven't had time to go through all the books yet," she answered. She was trying to keep her answers as truthful as possible. The guy had to be paranormal, although there was clearly a mix of human and paranormal in his minions. But you never knew who may be able to sense a lie. She had browsed through a couple of the books and there had been one that had caught her eye right away. Marge had only glanced at it before deciding to lock them all up in the protected room. She was glad she had because if she had to guess that was the book he was looking for.

"Because the library where it had been shipped it here. I managed to get that information out of the librarian before I killed her," he sneered at her.

Marge felt a pang of loss. There weren't very many of them in the paranormal community and she ached that they had lost a Guardian, although she was also a little pissed that they had told him where the book had been sent. Maybe they sent it here to keep it safe, maybe they had thought the wards would protect her as well? Being angry at a dead woman didn't do her any good, so she took a deep breath and let the anger go.

"Oh, don't worry. She kept her mouth shut, but I had a magical helper at the time. No one can hide the truth from my little friend over there." He pointed out a ratty-looking figure. The light didn't let her get a good look at them, so she couldn't tell if it was a child or simply a very short adult. They cowered away when Boss Guy pointed at them. She would have to keep an eye on them; she had a feeling they weren't there willingly. They weren't well dressed and didn't act like the others here. She couldn't remember seeing them at the library. Either way, Marge was now glad that she hadn't looked at the books closely yet. She was also glad that the library's wards were so strong. Even if they forced her to walk into the back room, there was no way they could force her to come out. She could also enact a spell that wouldn't allow the books to leave. The wards currently allowed her to remove materials if needed, although it didn't work that way for anyone else. If she uttered the spell, even she wouldn't be able to get the books through the wards.

"I'm not lying. I haven't gone through the books yet. That was supposed to happen today," Marge told him.

The slight figure nodded, confirming she was telling the truth.

"Hmm. I know it's there; we'll just have to get it out," he replied.

"Boss, there's some movement in town looking for her." A minion came running up, out of breath.

"Let's move farther in. Keep the necklaces on. We don't want them finding us before we get what we need from her."

Marge tried to brace herself, as she was pulled up to stand. Maybe she could hop away if they were distracted, she thought to herself. As soon as she was standing, she realized that wasn't going to happen yet. Her head pounded, her vision wavered, and her stomach heaved. She bent over, throwing up what little was left in her stomach. She clearly had a pretty bad head injury.

"Bring her," Boss Guy ordered.

The other paranormal, the one she thought had hit her back at the library, roughly dragged her up and threw her over his shoulder. "Vomit on me and I'll drop you to the ground and drag you the rest of the way," he threatened.

Marge clenched her teeth together, willing her stomach to settle. The motion and bouncing against his back certainly weren't helping. The smaller figure walked behind them. From here, Marge could see that it was a child, probably preteen in terms of age. They had a bracelet on, connected to a leash that attached to the belt of the man carrying her. The boy quickly glanced around before reaching out with a trembling finger. Marge moved her hand to meet him.

'*I'm sorry,*' the boy said telepathically.

Marge nodded, letting him know she heard him. She wasn't sure if she could respond telepathically, but the way her head was aching, she wasn't going to try right now. She tried to give him a small smile in response, but she had a feeling she passed out again before she managed it.

Marge woke up briefly, smelling and feeling dampness. The sunlight was no longer trying to stab her eyes, so either they were under cover, or the sun had set. Her feet were cold, and she realized that her boots and socks had been removed.

Barely opening her eyes, she looked around. There was a small fire burning in the center of the room. Guards were at the doorway. She was all the way in the back of what must be a cave. Her eyes were still a little blurry, but she could see damp stone walls. The ground beneath her was a mix of dirt and stone. She now had a bracelet on her wrist, her ankle cuffs had been reduced to one, but she was chained to the wall of the cave.

She heard motion next to her and involuntarily tensed.

'I won't hurt you,' the boy said. *'They're still arguing if we should stay here or not. If you keep still, they won't notice you.'*

Marge made an effort to connect with the boy, being mindful that this could still be a ploy to gain her trust. While her gut said he was a victim too, she would still be careful.

'Thanks. Where are we?'

The boy's eyes darted all around the room. *'In a cave. Never been in one before, just read about them in school.'*

'Did we go far from town?' she asked patiently.

'Not really. I think we're in the forest near the town. We walked here, we didn't drive.'

'How did you get here?' Marge asked. She figured if the boy was a victim, she could help him once she got free. If he was a plant, she probably wouldn't get too much out of him.

'They took me out of school. I went to a regular human school, and they came in dressed like police officers and had some papers that said they could take me. School just let me go, they didn't even call my mom or dad. Do you think they're okay?'

'I hope so. If we get free, I can help you look for them,' Marge replied.

"We're fine here. It's hidden well enough, there's plenty of wildlife around to eat. As long as you keep the blockers on, they won't be able to sense what you are. She has the bracelet on, so it's not like they can find her that way either. We're good. It's not far enough away that if we break her, it will take us long to get the book."

A pair of feet walked closer, and she kept her eyes shut, her breathing regular. A boot tapped her ribs none too gently, causing her to grunt.

"Wake up," Boss Guy said.

"What do you want?" she asked grumpily.

"I'm going to see if you're going to be any more cooperative. See that new little bracelet on your wrist? It's a Tamer spell. You won't be able to shift. It also has a lovely little side effect of blocking your increased healing. That means that anything we do to you, you won't be able to heal from. Gives us so much more fun; well, probably not for you," he said, both glee and derision in his voice. "It has a blocker spell as well, so whoever you think is going to rescue you, they won't. No one will be able to scent you. You're here until I'm tired of dealing with you. Even if you somehow get out of the chain, we've destroyed your shoes, so good luck walking to safety."

"I'm not going to let you in the library," she said. "I don't even have my keys with me."

"Does she not have her keys?" Boss Guy asked the boy.

"No. She doesn't have them. She'd have to ask the other employee to let her in, but that lady doesn't have the key to the locked room. She's also always with other paranormals," the boy added on.

Marge looked at him. That part wasn't entirely true. Merri went to the bakery and bookstore by herself quite a lot.

'I don't want them hurting your friend,' the boy told her quietly.

'Thank you,' Marge replied.

"We can still try to grab the lady," the huge guy spoke up. Marge was going to call him Minion One. He was some sort of paranormal; the strength he showed in the library wasn't human.

Boss Guy shook his head. "They're going to be on alert after her disappearance. We didn't have time to clean up the mess. They have a Warden in town as well and I don't want to have to deal with him. The other lady is useless if she doesn't have a key to the room we need.

"Let's see if a few days of no food changes your mind. If you want it bad enough, there's a way for you to get in that room."

3

Duncan was excited to visit Rockfort again. He hadn't gotten to see much of it the last time he was here. He had come to defeat the asshole who had killed his sister and once he helped with the clean-up, he had left. He had thought that helping make sure Vlad was dead and could no longer hurt anyone else would make him feel better, but it hadn't. Not really. He felt a little lighter, knowing that Hope had been avenged, but not as free as he thought he would. He honestly thought he would never come back to this small Tennessee town, but something had drawn him back. He had driven his motorcycle this time, clothes and phone charger in his saddlebags. He figured he'd stay long enough to see what he was supposed to see. He would have ignored it, but he'd had a dream where his sister told him to get his butt back here. If anyone could reach across the veil, she would have.

He stopped at the hotel first, checking in and bringing his bags to his room. He had traveled light and would need to stop at the store to get some drinks and toiletries. It was nice out today and he wondered if he would be able to fly tonight. Maybe he could ask Rolf if he could take off from his property so he wouldn't be seen changing. He had seemed like a nice guy when Duncan had met him before the fight. He hadn't known him personally before that day but had heard stories through the paranormal grapevine. The guy had the misfortune of having Vlad as a father, although he had turned out to be the complete opposite of his dad. When a mutual acquaintance had mentioned Rolf was recruiting people to help stand against Vlad, Duncan had jumped at the chance to hurt the guy who took his sister away from him. Their parents had been withdrawn and stopped talking to him after she died. They blamed him for not being home to protect her. It didn't seem to matter that she had been an adult on her own and he had already been gone from home for three hundred years when it had happened. When he angrily pointed that out, his father had taken a swipe at him. Unfortunately, he had been so angry that his claws had shifted, hence the scar by his right eye.

Hope had been his older sister, his only sibling, and they had always been close. He had felt the moment she died, terror running through her veins. With his parents curled up in their own grief, he had started to train knowing one day the opportunity would come where he could avenge his sibling. It took some effort to learn who had killed her. There had been witnesses, but they were afraid to speak up. He knew he would have a hard time doing it on his own, even being a dragon. Vlad surrounded himself with strong paranormal minions who would die to protect him. When Rolf's call for help had gone out, it was just the opportunity Duncan needed. He had carried his sister's amulet with him the day he helped kill the monster who took her life.

Shaking off his morose thoughts, Duncan grabbed his keys and wallet, deciding to walk to the grocery store. He bought a few nonperishable items to snack on, a case of water, instant coffee packets, and toiletries. He didn't know how long he would be here, but he could always buy more. Most of his stuff was in storage anyway. A flyer grabbed his attention as he walked out of the store. "Town Hall Security Meeting, Mandatory Attendance." Huh. It was posted by the Sheriff, who Duncan knew was also a paranormal Warden. Looked like that was in an hour. He had enough time to run his groceries back to the hotel, grab a quick snack and head to the meeting. While he didn't live here, he felt an urge to see if there was something he could do to help keep the town safe.

Walking to the meeting, he saw stores closed all along the way. It seemed like the townspeople were all going to be in attendance. He thought that was a little odd. You normally didn't get that much compliance with people, not without force. Rolf seemed like he had been protecting the town and he hadn't heard about anything happening to him, so he didn't think that someone else had taken over the town. He joined the crowds outside the doors. Gage, the Sheriff/Warden stepped out. He looked tired, Duncan thought.

"Thank you all for coming. We want to get your input on a situation you may have heard about. We're meeting in the basement and it's going to be a tight fit to get everyone in. We do have a room upstairs for children. Please consider having them go there; there's coloring pages, movies, snacks. We have Shaye, Sam, and Mary from the bakery in there to watch over them. There are some sensitive things we need to discuss that probably aren't appropriate for them," Gage said.

Duncan could hear the murmur that went through the crowd, but it seemed like parents were taking their children upstairs. He waited his turn, letting the townspeople go in before him. If there wasn't room, he would just talk to Gage later. Several minutes later, he made his way to the door.

"Sheriff." He nodded at him. "Mind if I attend the meeting?"

Gage stared, his eyes boring into him, searching for something. "You were at Rolf's last year in the Fall? Got that big bonfire started?"

Duncan was confused for a moment then realized that he

was talking about the fight. There were a lot of humans around and they had to watch what they said.

"That was me. Quite the night. Something pulled me back in for a visit," Duncan replied.

A shorter woman with long black curly hair pulled into a ponytail came over to Gage. "We're ready," she said softly. "I may go upstairs with the kids. There's too many people," she said. Duncan could hear the anxiety in her voice, her hands trembling a little.

"Do you want me to take you home? Or Doc can, he doesn't have to stay," Gage offered gently.

She shook her head firmly. "I need to stay. Marge is one of ours. I just can't be in that room with so many people. Albert will keep me updated."

Duncan realized this was Rolf's mom. He had heard stories about the things Vlad had put her through. No wonder she didn't want to be surrounded by so many people.

"Tell Doc if you need to leave," Gage said firmly.

"I will," Emma replied.

She looked at Duncan. "Hello again," she said quietly. "Thank you for your help last year. I don't think I got to tell you tha—" her voice cut off, her body swaying. Gage gently grabbed her.

"Is she okay?" Duncan asked worriedly. Her eyes were unfocused, and she wasn't responding to them. He startled, his body tensing for a fight when he felt a bolt of magic surge out of Gage, hitting him in the chest. It didn't hurt, just a tickling sensation over his whole body. Just as suddenly as it happened, it disappeared.

"Sorry. Had to make sure you were safe. She has visions," Gage replied as another man came running out from the stairway. The doctor, if he remembered correctly.

"What happened?" he demanded, taking Emma into his arms, his fingers finding her pulse.

"Vision," Gage replied.

Seconds later, Emma blinked and looked right at Duncan. "Let him in the meeting, Gage. He needs to be here. He'll help." She gave Duncan's arm a light pat. "It'll be fine," she promised.

"I'm going to take her home," Doc said.

"No. I'm going upstairs. I'll get a juice box and one of the cookies that are up there. You're going to the meeting," she replied firmly before giving Doc a kiss on the cheek and walking up the stairs, holding on to the railing for support.

"What was that?" Duncan asked, so very confused.

Gage sighed. "I really would like the town to be quiet again," he complained.

Doc nodded. "That would be nice. Duncan, right?" he asked.

Duncan nodded.

"Emma has visions and this one must have been about you."

"What will be fine?" he asked.

Doc shrugged. "She's not sharing the vision with me, so I'm not sure."

"What in the world is going on?" Duncan was sure he was missing something important.

"We've had a few issues since you were last here. I think we have a hunter problem," Gage said bluntly. "We can't find the bastards and it's driving me nuts. We have reason to believe they have some major support. I can fill you in later at Rolf's after the meeting if you want to come over. It's more secure there. Yesterday our librarian was taken. That's part of what the meeting is about."

Two more people came out before Duncan could respond. They looked familiar.

"We're ready, Gage. No one triggered the spell, so it should be safe. We're going to cast a silencing spell around the building. No one will be able to eavesdrop," the man said.

"Tess, Berkley, this is Duncan. You might remember him

helping with the bonfire last year at Rolf's. Emma invited him to stay," Gage introduced them. "I'll go make sure everyone is seated while you guys finish the spell. Doc, can you help Duncan find a seat?"

"Come on, Duncan. You can stand with the rest of us. I don't think there's an open seat in there," Doc replied.

As he followed him into the basement, Duncan had to wonder just what he had gotten himself into.

4

"Thank you for coming tonight," Gage started. Duncan watched the crowd, seeing Tess and Berkley slip in at the back.

"I'm going to let Rolf talk and then I'll jump in," Gage said.

Duncan watched as Rolf walked to the front, his throat swallowing a few times. He seemed nervous.

"I know a lot of you know me. Or Sam or Berkley or Doc. We've been around awhile." That drew a few laughs out of the crowd. Some just looked confused. "I've known most of your families for a long, long time. Some of you who only moved here recently, may not have noticed anything different about this town. Please bear with me while I tell a quick story. I promise it's the truth and it has to deal with what we're here about.

"I came here over a hundred years ago. I loved this area, made a home here. Sam and then Berkley joined me. I was close enough to get groceries and supplies in town to build my house, but far enough out of town that I thought no one would notice anything different about us. However, you guys were smart and picked up on it no matter how careful we were. Even when we left for years at a time, some of you still remembered us. We knew this was our home, so we helped protect it. You guys helped protect us too, keeping our secret."

Holy cow, Rolf was outing himself to the entire town. This was not how Duncan thought this would go. Looking around the room, Duncan could see several people in the crowd nodding. Some still looked confused.

"Something's come up and we need to get your input. You probably have guessed that we're not the only ones of our kind. Unfortunately, like with everything, not all of us are good. When I was sick last year, that was because someone tried to kill me. We took care of the problem with the help of the Sheriff. However, something is brewing, and it might affect you," Rolf said.

"How the heck can he be over a hundred? He's like thirty or something," Duncan heard someone whisper.

"I'm actually a little over two hundred years old," Rolf replied calmly. It was obvious he had heard them when a normal person wouldn't have been able to.

"I think you might need help. No one lives that long," the man replied.

"Just be quiet and listen," another man replied.

"Bill, you can't be serious. This guy needs some mental help. Why are we even listening to this?"

"I've known Rolf my entire life. Doc delivered me. He's not making anything up, he's not crazy. Just listen," Bill said.

There were a few mutters in the crowd by the ones who had looked confused. Duncan would guess these were the newer residents who didn't know they were living among paranormals.

Rolf sighed. "Okay. There are people out in the world who aren't exactly human. Some of them started human like I did. Others were born that way. Most of us just want to live our lives, and we try to live amongst everyone peacefully."

"If you're not human, then what are you?" the man in the crowd interrupted again.

"Paranormals. We're a varied bunch that call this town home. I'm a vampire, there are a few witches, some shifters. I'm not going to call them out by name, that's up to them to share. But there are several of us here. This has been a safe place to live and in exchange, we help watch over the town and keep it safe."

"Prove it," the man demanded.

Duncan shook his head. Everyone always wanted proof. People asked, not really believing in the slightest that it could be real before they asked for proof, and then panicking afterward when their minds had trouble processing what they had seen. Stupid movies and their portrayals of paranormals; they were always made out to be the bad guys.

Rolf nodded. Duncan could feel a slight shift in the air before Rolf opened his mouth to show his fangs.

"Those could be fake," the man protested.

Duncan rolled his eyes. This was going to take forever. There wasn't enough room for him to shift in here though.

"Ever see a large black dog or a wolf running in the woods? That's me," Sam said.

"Or it's Emma's new dog or another big dog," the man countered. "Turn into a wolf then."

Sam's cheeks turned red. "Well, I have to get naked to shift, and I don't think you want to see that."

"That's convenient."

Duncan almost spoke up when Bill smacked the guy's arm. "Stop being an ass."

The guy with the white stripe in his hair stepped forward. "I'm a different kind of shifter. I don't need to undress to change, if you really need to see it."

"Sure, go ahead," the man scoffed. "Oh, fuck," he whispered when there was suddenly a peregrine falcon standing where a man had been.

Duncan would guess that he would try to say it was a trick. The shifter must have thought the same thing because he flew right at the man. Bill stood up and moved over to give him room. The shifter tapped the man's leg gently with his beak, making him feel he was real. Then suddenly there was a man standing next to him, the bird nowhere to be seen.

"This is crazy. You expect us to just accept this as normal and want to live near a bunch of monsters?"

Duncan wondered if any of the paranormals in the room had the ability to erase memories. This guy had the potential to be a huge dick. If they did have a problem with hunters, they wouldn't want someone blabbing about paranormals living in the town.

"Ninety-five percent of the people here already believed them. We've known them our whole lives, heard the stories passed down from our grandparents, great grandparents, sometimes great-great grandparents. Rolf helped save our land, he let us hunt and cut down trees on his own property when the government took land for the National Park and banned those activities. A lot of our ancestors relied on hunting and the timber to live. They would have starved or had to move if it hadn't been for him. Over the years, I think he's helped everyone in this town. Even you, Steve," Bill pointed out.

Steve laughed. "Sure he did. How?"

"It's fine, Bill," Rolf said. "He doesn't have to be comfortable with the idea right away."

Bill shook his head. "My Mary would be upset if I didn't speak up. Of course, she would have already banned him from the bakery with talk like that," he joked. He turned to Steve with a serious look. "Take your accident three years ago. You lost your job because you were a contractor and couldn't work for months while you recovered, couldn't pay the mortgage or the hospital bills. They were sending debt collectors after you, and threatening foreclosure."

"Yeah, that's what I get for working for a big company and going through an online bank for the mortgage. They don't care about you," Steve responded.

"Suddenly, you got a call saying there was an insurance policy the company had on its contract employees, and it was enough to pay off your bills and get your mortgage up to date. There had even been enough money after that to make sure you could pay the mortgage while you looked for another job. And the bank offered you a better interest rate, so you ended up paying less on your mortgage going forward," Bill pointed out.

"Yeah, so?"

"There was no insurance policy. Rolf takes care of this town. Everyone in this town. None of the kids who grow up here pay for college. They all receive full scholarships to whatever college they applied to. No one loses their home or car, no one goes hungry. He has things set up for pretty much any scenario. If he knows you well enough, he'll give it to you directly. If he doesn't, like with you, he'll find a way to help. The rest of the paranormals here help protect the town in their own way as well. I'm not going to out them either, but all of them have literally bled to keep the town safe over the years," Bill said before taking his seat again.

There were a lot of nods in the crowd.

"Why? Does he eat us and that's his way of feeling good about it?"

Good lord this man was stupid, Duncan thought. Rolf just burst out laughing.

"No, I don't drink from anyone in town. I use blood bags. I don't get diseases, so I can use the blood that the hospital can't. I eat regular food and don't need to drink that often," Rolf told him. "And to answer what is probably your next question; no, a bite doesn't turn someone into a vampire. A vampire would have to want to turn you when they bit you. Simply drinking from you won't do it."

Gage sent a look to the back of the room to Berkley and Tess. Berkley nodded. Gage stepped forward.

"I've been Sheriff here a while. It's my job, and my joy, to keep this town safe. In addition to being your Sheriff, I'm a Warden. A paranormal police officer of sorts. I keep the town and surrounding areas safe from paranormals who aren't quite as nice as the ones that live here. Just like with regular humans, there are good and bad paranormals. A human honestly doesn't have a chance against most paranormals, so Wardens are in charge of areas to keep humans safe. The majority of us really do just want to live our lives, peacefully.

"Unfortunately, there has been a resurgence of hunters across the world. Some of them seem to be linked to a paranormal group. Hunters kill or capture paranormals. Sometimes it's to sell, sometimes it's to torture, to sell as a science experiment. There have been signs of them nearby. Flyers from a so-called author looking to collect local stories, myths, and legends for a new book. He even pays for the stories, extra for any proof. He wants to know if there have been any weird occurrences, animal bites, things like that. So far, in every town where these flyers have shown up, people have gone missing. No one has been able to find them. Their families don't know if they're dead or taken. We believe they are working with a paranormal group because they have been using spells to keep us from tracking them. There have been signs of people camping in the National Park, but we can't track their scents.

"Sometime Monday night, Marge, our town librarian was taken. I hate to say this without her permission, but it's relevant to this meeting. She's a shifter. There was clearly a struggle and we found blood at the scene. I called in a tracker, but he can't follow them as they used a blocker of some sort. She should have been able to hold her own against a human or two, so either it was a lot of humans, or they were paranormals, or a mix. We're trying to find her. I didn't expect them to make a move like that in town, not with so many people nearby.

"So here is what we called the meeting for. We would like to place a spell over the town. It's taken us a long time to get the wording correct, but we finally have it. The spell would keep ill-intentioned people out. If you came to town wanting to hurt someone whether they were human or paranormal, the wards wouldn't let you in. If you're a violent person, the wards will keep you out. Everyone loses their temper, it's not for that kind of anger. If you beat your wife, the wards will keep you out. If you are a hunter looking to capture or kill a paranormal, the wards will keep you out. If you're already in town, the wards will push you out. This effects the whole town and we wanted to put it to a vote."

"Why don't you all just leave?" Steve asked belligerently.

"Well, we were here long before you moved here," Sam answered. "If we leave, there's still no guarantee that the hunters would leave as well. Or that they'll leave you alone and not try to get information from you."

"I don't see how this is a bad thing. It's protecting the whole town?" a woman in the back asked.

Gage nodded. "The whole town. We have it planned to cover everyone's properties, even the farms, not just the main downtown area."

"I'm for it," another man spoke up. "After all, you could just protect your own and leave us to fend for ourselves. Keeping us safe seems like a mighty nice thing to do," he said, staring at Steve.

Steve sat there, not saying anything. Duncan watched him as the town voted. He was the only one to not raise his hand in support. He didn't vote no either, so Duncan wasn't sure what that meant.

"Thank you," Gage said. "Our plan is to initiate it within the next day or two. If you are out and hear anyone talking about things we went over or see one of the flyers, please tell us. If you hear anything about Marge, or if you saw anything weird or out of place last night, please let us know. The library will be closed for the foreseeable future. It's being treated as a crime scene. If you have any questions, please come ask. Thank you for your time," Gage concluded.

Duncan watched as Berkley formed some sort of spell. He would have to ask what it was later. He would guess it was to keep an eye on Steve. It took another hour or so until the room cleared out.

"Do you want to come back to the house for dinner?" Rolf asked. "Mom put some soups in the crockpots this morning and Tess made some bread."

"Sure, that sounds good," Duncan replied. It had been a while since he had shared a meal with anyone, much less a homemade meal surrounded by other paranormals. "Let me grab my bike and I'll head over."

"We can give you a ride, if you want," Sam offered.

"Thanks." Duncan followed them out to their cars, Gage following in the police SUV.

Pulling up to the gates, Duncan was hit with just how different this time entering Rolf's area was.

Dinner was delicious and it was nice to get to know everyone a little better. There was quite the range of paranormals and personalities. He waited until everyone was done eating to bring up the meeting again.

"What have I missed since the last time I was here? It seems like there's more backstory to the meeting tonight."

"Marge is our town librarian, but she is also the Guardian of the Library. The entire back room is one of the paranormal libraries. There are several scattered about, but they're relatively rare. She holds the only key to that room and there are a lot of wards in place to keep that room safe. We got a shipment of books from an unknown source. Marge was going to try to reach out to her fellow librarians and some contacts and see if anyone had sent them to her. There was no return address. We locked them in the back room, and I left for the day. We were going to work on them yesterday. I got to the library early so we could get to work and found the door locked. I couldn't hear her inside. When the guys arrived, we found signs of a struggle and blood. Some was Marge's, some belonged to someone else. We checked around town, trying to find any trace of them. Gage brought in a Tracker, but even he couldn't find anything. We wanted to put the spell over the town but didn't want to do it without letting them know the dangers and why we were doing it. It really shouldn't affect them, everyone has been nice since I've been here," Merri told him.

"Do you think they're hiding in town or somewhere else?" Duncan asked.

"My best guess is somewhere else," Gage answered. "I think someone would have mentioned guests at the hotel or the bed and breakfast."

"They didn't mention me," Duncan pointed out.

"You were also standing up there with us."

Emma grabbed Doc's hand. "She's in the woods."

Rolf looked at his mother. "You heard that too?"

"Heard what?" Doc asked.

"Hm. How to describe it…it was the equivalent to a telepathic shout. Someone who doesn't have a lot of experience or training in using it. It was more of an image really, showing Marge in the woods."

"Why didn't the rest of us get it?" Sam asked.

"Mom and I have telepathy as a natural gift, not one from bonds. We could project into anyone who wasn't shielded properly. And we do keep our shields up, plus the wards here would keep out any that were meant in a harmful way. The caster must have been desperate and put a lot of energy and emotion behind it," Rolf answered.

"Are you sure it wasn't Marge doing it?"

Rolf shook his head. "She was in the image, and it didn't feel like her, if that makes any sense."

Duncan found himself speaking up. "I can do a flyover if you think she's nearby. I can try to sense anyone in the woods and look for anything out of place."

"That would be amazing," Gage said. "We've found traces of people clearly camping in the woods, but we can't trace them. It's leaving us at a disadvantage."

"I can go right now," he offered.

5

Duncan had flown over the woods for over two hours last night, coming back to crash in one of the extra rooms at Rolf's house. He could sense something in the woods, but he now knew what they meant when they said they couldn't trace it. He could even see some blood on the ground in one spot, but something had been sprayed on it and there was no scent remaining. His dragon was furious, but he wasn't exactly sure why. It was frustrating knowing the lady was out there somewhere and he couldn't use his senses to find her.

Today he was going to meet Merri at the library so he could get Marge's scent. He was hoping that would help him track her, but if the Warden couldn't do it, he didn't hold much hope he could. Gage had told them they could go in today. He had finished collecting evidence and the Clan was going to help get it cleaned up for when Marge came home. They weren't even considering the fact that she might not come back. This was a great group of people, and his dragon was already making noise about roosting here. He didn't have any relatives left and he wondered if his sister had pushed him here to find a family. The Nightwood Clan were welcoming of all types of paranormals, and he felt comfortable around them. He thought that they could be friends. Duncan briefly wondered if there were any good places to hide a hoard.

There was a knock on the bedroom door just as he finished brushing his teeth.

Opening it, he found Berkley. "Morning. I just wanted to let you know that breakfast is ready, if you're hungry. It's just a few of us this morning; Doc and Shaye already left to go to the clinic, Sam had an early delivery he had to be there to sign for, and Merri and Emma are already on the way to the library."

"Breakfast sounds great," Duncan replied. He followed Berkley down the stairs. He caught glimpses into other rooms as they went. If Rolf had been a dragon, books would have been his hoard, Duncan thought with a laugh. That was one huge library. It spanned both floors from what he could tell.

"Thanks for letting me crash here last night," he told Rolf when he saw him in the kitchen.

"No problem. Thank you for taking a look. I had an idea, and feel free to say no," Rolf started. He looked at Tess, who nodded. "Why don't you stay here? It's a safe spot and you'll have use of the woods and the land if you need to stretch your wings. If you'd rather stay at the hotel, you're still welcome to use the property."

"That would be nice," Duncan replied. It was nice here and it would save him some money, although he would contribute to the groceries. He could eat a lot. "May I ask why?" Not that he didn't believe the offer was genuine, but he also knew Rolf wasn't in the habit of asking random paranormals to stay in his house.

Tess spoke up. "There's a couple of reasons. You helped us before. We know you're safe."

Duncan interrupted. "How do you know I'm safe? Because I helped you before?"

Berkley smiled. "No. Emma's vision showed her a bit of who you are. Mostly though, the wards let you through. The wards here have been enforced by witch, Fae, and shifter magic. No one who means harm is getting through. Not by foot, by air, or even by digging."

Duncan remembered seeing the decorative carvings on the doorways and realized that those were part of the wards. "That's some magic you guys have going on," he said.

"We learned the hard way," Rolf said dryly.

Oh yeah, he remembered hearing about him being poisoned from a blood supply that had been brought to the house. Man, that had to have sucked. It took a lot to poison a vampire and to do it in the safety of his own home was extra cruel.

"The wards meant you were welcome here, but I had a dream last night. Emma has her visions while she's awake. I sometimes have ones in dreams. Anyway. It's your choice, but my dream showed you as one of us. If you'd like."

"What does that mean?" he asked cautiously. He thought they were offering a place in the Nightwood Clan, but he wanted it to be clear.

Tess shook her head. "Sorry, that wasn't very clear, was it? I blame it on the fact I haven't finished my coffee yet," she laughed. "My vision showed you as part of the Nightwood Clan, if you would like."

"We're a pretty good group, if I do say so myself," Rolf said with a smile. "So far, we all live here, but we're pretty relaxed, so if you wanted to live in town or up in the mountains that would be fine too. Your mate would be welcome as well when you find them. I don't collect tithes like some Clans do. I only ask that anyone who joins be welcoming and accepting, of humans and paranormals."

"We all just help with the groceries and chores around the house," Berkley added.

Duncan nodded. It was something he hadn't been expecting. At best he had been thinking they would be a good group of people to be friends with. He actually loved the fact that they accepted all different types of paranormals. His parents had been more of the "stick to your own kind" and had isolated themselves. There weren't a lot of dragons around. When his sister died, there was no one else there to support them and they had kicked him out. After the fight where his dad had lashed out in anger, he went back thirty years later figuring they would have calmed down. Instead, he found their skeletons curled around each other. They had just given up and without a community to support them, no one had been there to force them to live. He still felt guilty for not checking in sooner even though they hadn't wanted him there. This group of friends would never let someone go without support. He had a feeling it didn't matter if he joined and moved to Alaska, they would find a way to help him if he needed it.

Tess poked Rolf, tilting her head at Duncan.

"Oh! Yeah, thanks for reminding me," Rolf told her.

Duncan was a little confused as she hadn't said anything.

"No one outside of the Clan other than Gage knows this. Our Clan has a special bond. Sam was injured and due to a spell, he couldn't be healed with witch-based magic. It was a death spell, and we were desperate to save him. Our research gave us nothing solid until Gawain remembered about the old-school blood bonds. It was what allowed us to save Sam. It's a bond that is so hard to break, it's pretty permanent. There's an oath you take, I accept you into the Clan and bite you, and the bond forms. We're all telepathically linked to each other. Which tends to be helpful, since we keep running into trouble," Rolf added.

"That last time would hae been me," Ian said as he walked into the room. "We were attacked when we were in Scotland. The bond allowed them to help heal me."

Duncan had a feeling there was more to the story, but he

understood them not telling him all of their secrets since he hadn't agreed to join the Clan yet.

"Can I have some time to think about it? Either way, I'll keep your secret," Duncan promised. His dragon was pushing him to say yes, but his human side was more cautious.

"Of course. We just wanted to let you know you were welcome. Either way you decide, you're welcome to stay at the house instead of paying for the hotel room."

"I'd love to stay. I just need a little time to think about the other offer," he said.

Rolf nodded. "No problem."

"If ye want to grab your stuff while you're in town, we can bring it back in the SUV," Ian offered.

"I don't have much with me right now, it all fits in my saddlebags. If I decide to move here, I'll have to get some things out of storage."

"Give me a few minutes, and I'll be ready to go," Ian said as he gave Berkley a light kiss.

"I'll grab you some food," Berkley said.

"Thanks, love," Ian said, giving him another kiss before walking out.

"I'm going to run upstairs for my wallet and phone. I'll be right back down," Duncan said.

It was nice being so close to town even though the house felt like it was its own little world. When they pulled up to the library, he could see the police sign on the front door stating it was closed until further notice. He got out with Rolf, Tess, Ian, and Berkley and walked to the front door. Rolf knocked and his mate opened the door with a large wolfdog by her side.

"What are you doing here? I thought you were at work," Rolf asked, bending down to give her a kiss on the cheek.

"I'm going back in a few minutes. I had a feeling I needed to be here when you arrived," Shaye said with a small shrug.

"Hey, Rockefeller. Good boy for protecting my mate," Rolf praised him. The large dog pressed his head into Rolf's hand and then greeted the rest of his family.

"Let's go find your mama," Sam said.

The dog spun around and took off.

"That is a huge dog. Wolfdog, right?" Duncan asked.

Sam nodded. "Emma and Doc found him when he was tiny. His mother had been shot. We're thinking it was hunters. The paranormal kind because it was in the National Park, and we didn't catch a scent near her. Human hunters would have left some sort of trace, even if it was covered with a layer of deer urine or whatever they use to cover their natural scent when hunting. We have no idea how she came to be in the forest; we don't really have wolves here. He had enough dog in his scent that we could raise him. He's been a great addition to the family."

Berkley shut and locked the door behind them.

Duncan's dragon tried to take over, fury pouring out of him. The scent of blood was strong in the air.

Shaye rushed to lay her hand on his arm, his skin already shining with his scales. He could feel the calming vibes she was trying to project.

"Duncan, don't. You'll destroy her library. Hold it together until you're outside," she urged.

Rolf had tensed beside him. "What's wrong?"

"Marge is my mate."

6

Marge felt little hands gently shaking her leg.

'Marge, you gotta wake up,' he said fearfully. *'Please don't be dead.'*

She opened her eyes a sliver, seeing the boy crouched in front of her. It seemed like the cave was pretty empty. The others must be outside. Boss Guy had been here last night and when she still wouldn't give him what he wanted, he had lost his temper. If she thought it was bad from the library attack, she must be really broken now. She knew her shoulder was still dislocated, but she thought there was a break somewhere in that arm as well. Her knee felt shattered, and her head had taken several hits. She couldn't remember most of it, but she remembered them holding the boy back as he tried to get to her, him screaming at them to stop and crying. When the beating stopped, they injected her with something that made her veins burn. She couldn't even feel her cat any longer.

Her face felt wet, but she couldn't muster the energy to brush it away.

'You're bleeding again,' he told her worriedly.

'Has there been any sign of the dragon again or anyone else in

the woods?' Marge asked, using telepathy, driving spikes of pain into her brain. She pushed through it because there was no way they could have a conversation aloud. She had been awake enough yesterday to hear the panicked voices when they realized there was a dragon flying overhead. They had seen it twice now and the minions were worried the dragon had been brought in to look for her.

Boss Guy told them not to be imbeciles and it was just a dumb shifter flying around. However, she didn't remember seeing him after that, just his minions. The boy had told her that he was part of the Convocation, so maybe he had work today or something. Or the dragon had spooked him.

The boy shook his head.

'I really thought they would have caught the scent of my blood and followed it to us by now,' she admitted.

'They had someone spraying something behind us the entire way. I don't think there's a scent left for them to find.'

Marge felt any hope leave her at that news. It probably shouldn't have surprised her. She felt like giving up, but she didn't want to leave the boy on his own. She wanted him to be free of these people. She wished she could remember what his name was. He had told her a couple of times, but she kept forgetting.

She thought she drifted off again but came back when he shook her.

'Here, drink this. I don't have a lot, but it rained for a couple of minutes last night and the wall is dripping with water,' the boy said, holding an old collapsible camping cup with a few swallows of water in it. He had tried sharing his meager rations with her but had gotten a beating for it. They now made him eat far away from her, but he had found the cup when he had a bathroom break in the woods and had snuck it in. There was a tiny trickle of water along the back wall of the cave. Which probably was why her lungs felt horrible. Or maybe it was her ribs causing the issue.

'Can you get some of my blood on your shoes or your hand and smear it around outside? Tell them you have to pee or something. It can be hidden under leaves, my friends will still smell it,' Marge asked. *'If they can scent me, they'll find me. I know they will.'* She was absolutely positive they were looking for her. She may not have known them for long as friends, but she knew down to her bones they were the ride or die kind.

The boy chewed on his lip, fear and worry chasing across his face before he finally nodded. He stepped close to her head, almost to the point where he was touching her. She moved her head back a little so he could get a trace on his shoe. Bending down to retie his shoe, he ripped a piece of his shirt off, soaking up as much of her blood as he could before he moved away from her and as close to the front of the cave as his leash allowed.

"I need to pee," he announced.

Minion One, the large paranormal, grumbled about how he just went out three hours ago but came over to unchain him. "Let's go, make it quick."

Marge watched as he left the cave. She hoped it would help Gage find her. She was going to get the boy out too. Hopefully his parents were missing him, and he could be reunited with them. If they were in cahoots with this group, she would find him a new home, with her if needed, although living in a library might not be that exciting for him.

'I found some berries,' he told her when he came back, sitting next to her as they chained him in place again. *'You need to eat something.'*

'I don't know that I can keep it down,' she admitted. Her stomach had been nauseous anytime she moved. Even the small sips of water she just had weren't sitting easy.

'Try, please,' he begged, slipping her a couple berries. She sniffed them, her cat still muted and not communicating if they were poisonous or not. She tried to make her brain focus and sort through all the knowledge she had of poisonous

plants in the area. She had given a talk at the school about this for goodness sake. Holding one close to her swollen eye, she thought it was a safe berry.

Marge managed to eat three before her stomach rebelled. She managed to roll over to her 'bathroom' area before she vomited. There was searing pain as she felt a broken rib move and puncture a lung. She could only hope that they arrived in time to save the boy. It was probably too late for her.

Duncan was beyond frustrated. Shaye had helped him control his dragon enough until he was out of the library. Then all bets were off. His beast ripped through him, taking to the sky with no care that it was daylight and anyone in town could see him. He flew over the forest all day, searching for his mate. His dragon roaring in frustration when he couldn't find her. He knew she was down there somewhere; he could feel it. Whatever blockers they were using were still keeping him from catching her scent.

By the time he landed in the Clan's backyard, he could barely walk. He hadn't eaten since breakfast, not stopping in his search until his wings threatened to give out. Ian had taken his keys and grabbed his bike and supplies from the hotel room.

Today he was in a fighting mood but was doing his best to avoid the people who had offered him a home. He didn't want to take it out on them.

He was brooding up in the third story of the library. He sat in the window seat, trying to think of what else to do.

"Hope, can you help? Give me a clue where to look? You sent me here. I thought it was to find a family, but now I know it was because my mate was here. Although maybe it was for family too," he added, holding on to his sister's pendant.

"Duncan?" a voice asked softly. Looking down, he saw Shaye standing at the bottom of the ladder. "Can you come down to the main floor library? We had an idea." He could tell she was pumping out the calming vibes again and his dragon relaxed a little in her presence. He gave her a nod before descending the ladder and following her down the stairs. Everyone was gathered around a huge table, the chairs moved off to the side.

"Okay, Emma and I both had the same vision. We don't know exactly where she is, but she's still in the woods. They've moved to a cave, so it's going to be hard to see from the air," Tess said.

"We've explored these woods quite a bit over the years," Rolf said. "We're marking the areas we know have caves. We can call in Gage and start searching each one. I think we need to go in groups since we don't know how many hunters there are."

Duncan nodded. He could take out a lot of hunters on his own with dragon fire, but the rest of them didn't have that option. He looked at the map. There were quite a few spots marked. He didn't realize there were so many caves in the area.

"We're also going to enact the spell over the town today. I have a feeling we're going to find her soon and I want her safe once we do. I don't want to take a chance of them coming back for her. Gage is coming over to help," Tess said.

"I'll help. I have some magic I can lend," Duncan offered. He had never had enough to really do anything with, but he could lend what he had.

"Thanks. It's going to be a doozy and I think we'll need everyone. It's a big area to surround. It's going to be similar to the one here, in that it will completely surround the town, both underground and in the air."

"What about that Steve guy? Do you think it's going to push him out?" Duncan asked. He hadn't heard anything more about the guy, but he certainly hadn't been happy to learn about paranormals at the town meeting.

"I hope not, but if it does, Berkley cast a spell that will cause him to forget about paranormals if he tries to tell someone outside of town. I'll make sure he gets all his assets transferred to another city and he gets another job, but at least he won't be a danger to us any longer," Rolf replied.

Duncan thought that was nicer than the guy deserved. He hadn't even said thank you to Rolf once even after he knew that he had been the one to take care of the guy's medical bills and mortgage problems.

The doorbell rang and they headed downstairs to let Gage inside.

"Let's go in the backyard," Tess suggested, holding a journal of some sort.

They gathered around the picnic table as she opened the notebook. "This is the spell," she said, showing them the page. Pulling out a map from the back of the book, she laid it down, showing an outline of the town. "Berkley, Gage, and I will be casting the spell, but if you all hold on to us and channel any magic you have through us, the spell will be stronger and hopefully be easier to cast," Tess said.

As they lined up, Duncan placed his hand on Berkley's left shoulder, Ian holding on to his mate's right shoulder. He could feel the air thicken, the hairs on his arms standing straight up as the magic grew. He focused on pushing what magic he had into the spell, holding on to the hope that he would find his mate and this would help protect her. He almost lost focus when he felt how strong Gage's magic was, but he made himself pay attention to his own thread, seeing it join with the others. He could tell they were saying words, but his ears were buzzing with the amount of magic being gathered and he couldn't make out what was being said. Suddenly it shot into the air, spreading out like an umbrella, falling down to the ground. He turned his head, seeing a dome being formed on all sides. The earth shook as the spell met in the middle underground, completing the circle and sealing itself together. He grabbed onto Berkley as he felt him stumble.

Emma ran inside with Shaye, bringing back cookies, nuts, and juice. "Everyone get a quick snack, you used a lot of energy," she said.

Duncan felt tired, so he couldn't imagine how drained the casters must be. Gage ate several cookies and was about to leave when Duncan's dragon stirred, scenting the air.

"Do you guys smell that?" Duncan asked.

They all shook their heads. "What is it?" Gage asked.

Duncan closed his eyes, bringing his dragon forward and drew a deep breath. Mate!

"I smell her!" he yelled.

"Can you track her?" Gage asked.

"I think so. Rolf, I want to initiate the Clan bond." His dragon was ready to go, but he knew he might need help.

"Are you sure? It's almost impossible to break. We'll help you either way."

"I'm sure. I can tell you where to go and get her help a lot faster. I wanted to anyway," he replied firmly, his dragon already pushing his scales out.

He felt Rolf initiate the telepathic link. '*I pledge fealty to my Clan leader, Rolfston of the Nightwood Clan,*' Duncan vowed, turning his head to offer his neck.

Rolf bit down, gentler than Duncan had anticipated. '*I accept you into my Clan,*' Rolf replied.

As soon as Duncan felt the bond snap into place, he ran further into the yard so his dragon didn't smoosh his new family, jumping into the air, he shifted, his wings beating hard to get him airborne.

He tracked the scent of his mate, sending images back over the Clan link so his family could follow.

7

Duncan flew, pushing himself to fly faster than he ever had. It was just the barest scent of his mate, and he didn't think he would have noticed if his dragon didn't already know what she smelled like. Tracking it to where the scent was the strongest only took minutes. He circled the area, looking for a cave entrance. From up here he couldn't see anything that resembled a cave, but he suddenly saw movement, the scurrying of little ants trying to hide.

He dove down, landing in front of them. He could see the entrance to the cave now, it wasn't very large, but it must open up. He could scent his mate's injuries and peered one eye into the cave. Seeing his mate unconscious, bleeding, and her breath labored, his dragon took over, breathing dragon fire to kill all those who dared harm her.

Duncan heard noises behind him and spun, ready to defend his mate.

"Easy, Duncan. It's just us," Rolf told him, the power of his voice as the Clan leader calming his dragon. "Go see to your mate. We'll see if there's anyone else here."

Gage had already started walking around the bodies.

"This one's still alive. I'm going to have Marco take him. Maybe we can get some information out of him."

Duncan startled as another man suddenly appeared. "Nice roasting," he said approvingly before disappearing with the man.

Ian rushed in. "I ran miles in all directions. There's no one else here."

Duncan changed, his dragon content to let go now that their family was here to back him up. Entering the cave, his steps faltered when he saw his mate. Her face was bruised, a swollen knot on the side of her head, blood and a clear fluid leaking from her. Her shoulder sat wrong, as did her wrist. Her left knee was so swollen, he was surprised it hadn't ripped the seams of the pants she was wearing. She had moved, curled up around something.

"Marge? I'm here to bring you home," he said softly. "The Nightwood Clan is outside. We've been looking for you. I don't know if you can hear me, but you're my mate. I'm so happy we found you." He tried to sound calm, he didn't want to scare her any more than she probably already was.

Her body moved, but she didn't answer. Moving closer, he gasped as a small body pulled itself out from under her.

"She won't wake back up," the boy said, fear in his voice. "When you roared and breathed fire, she woke up enough to pull me down and wrap around me. But now I can't get her to wake up. Are you really her mate? Is there anyone else left outside?"

Duncan found himself answering even though he hadn't planned on it. Shit, the kid must be a TruthSpeaker.

"I am her mate. Only one guy lived but a Warden we trust took him away for questioning. The only ones out there are our friends, the Nightwood Clan, and the local Warden."

Gage rushed in. "Where did that magic come from?"

"It seems Marge wasn't the only one they were keeping," Duncan replied, moving so Gage could see the boy.

Gage's magic flared, strong enough that even Duncan flinched. The boy dropped back to the ground, hiding behind Marge. "He's clean," Gage said. "He's not aligned with the hunters. I'm sorry, but I had to check to keep us all safe," he told the boy softly.

Duncan crouched by Marge's unconscious body, unsure how to move her. Ian rushed in, Shaye on his back. She jumped off, running to Marge. "We need to get her to the house. I don't know that I'll be able to fix all of this in one go. I'll stabilize her ribs and heal her lung, so they won't cause more problems when we move her, but we really need to get her to the house as soon as possible. Doc's setting up the room now."

"I can fly her back," Duncan offered, watching as Shaye laid a hand on Marge. "If someone can carry her out and put her in my claws, I'll fly back. It'll be faster and less jarring than running."

"I'll run Shaye back as soon as she's done here," Ian offered.

"We'll finish up here and meet you there," Rolf added.

"Don't forget the boy," Duncan said. "You'll be safe, these are Marge's friends. You can see her again at the house, okay?" he told the boy.

The boy gave a small, frightened nod, chewing nervously on his bottom lip.

"Let's move," Shaye said as she stood up. Ian squatted down for her to climb onto his back.

Gage bent to pick up Marge. "Oh, my friend, what did they do?" he whispered. Duncan hurried out of the cave, everyone already off to one side to give him room to shift. Gage walked over and gently placed her in his hand, his claws curling to hold her securely.

"Wait a minute. That's not one of her bracelets," Gage said angrily. He placed a hand over the metal. "Goddamn it. It's a Tamer spell. Berkley can you help me undo this?"

Duncan watched as they worked a spell together, a blinding light flared as the bracelet fell to the ground. The boy snuck closer.

"They gave her a shot yesterday. I don't know what it was," the boy said.

"I'll look at it," Shaye replied.

Duncan tried to have a gentler takeoff than normal, not wanting to jar her too much. Ian took off running so fast that Duncan couldn't see him. That must have been why he volunteered to take Shaye back, his gift was speed.

It only took minutes, but it felt like hours before he coasted to a stop in the backyard. Ian was there, ready to take Marge from his claws. Once he shifted, Ian gently transferred Marge and they rushed through the house, Shaye leading the way to a medical room. Doc was already in there, IVs ready to be used, bandages, and other things laid out.

Shaye sat in the chair next to the bed. Duncan registered that Tess, Merri, Emma, and Ian were standing back toward the door, but his sole focus was on his mate. In the bright light of the room, she looked even worse. Her hair was matted, tangled. It looked like it was soaked through with blood. There were spots where it looked like her hair had been ripped out. Bruises covered her body. Doc started to cut her pants away, Duncan's dragon letting out a growl.

"You have to control yourself," Doc told him firmly. "We don't have time for your beast to throw a hissy fit. I have my own mate," he reminded him.

"Sorry," Duncan apologized, ashamed that he had treated his new family and the people trying to help his mate that way.

'Her lung is still a little damaged, but I'm saving that for later. Dad, you probably want antibiotics. I can see an infection growing. The cave wasn't the best place for her injuries. I'm going to work on the big things first and see where we get. Dad, can you work on

cuts, the antibiotics, things like that?' Shaye asked. Duncan startled, her lips didn't move, but he could hear her clearly.

"It's the Clan link," Doc explained. "It's less effort for her to do it this way during a healing. She's also sending me images of what's wrong with Marge. Based on what Shaye's showing me, this will probably be two sessions. I'll work on the easier things like the antibiotics, stitches, setting her shoulder back in place. Shaye will work on the life-threatening things."

He helped Doc remove Marge's pants, wincing when he saw her knee. He pushed down the growl as Doc cut away Marge's shirt. Her torso was just one huge bruise.

"Duncan, take these wipes and clean off as much as you can. Work on her lower half but try not to move her. Shaye's focusing on her brain right now." Doc handed him a container of medical bath wipes. He knew he was being given busy work, but he was grateful to have something to do. Out of the corner of his eye, he saw Doc clean off one of her hands and start an IV. It looked like fluids and antibiotics.

"Shit," Doc muttered. He moved to hold Marge's head as she started waking up. Tess stepped forward.

"Sleep," she said gently, placing a drop of liquid on Marge's head. She looked at Duncan. "It's a simple sleeping spell and should only last an hour, but it will let Shaye and Doc work without disturbing her."

"That's it, Shaye, right there is where you need to focus. Get the swelling down first or the bones won't heal right. As it starts to shrink, keep an eye on any bone fragments, making sure they don't puncture anything," Doc guided as he kept a hand on Marge's head.

As Duncan watched, he began to see a difference in Marge's face. The clear fluid that had been leaking slowed down and then stopped, the blood flow also slowed, but still sluggishly bled from the cuts themselves. He didn't know anything about her healing gift, but Shaye was looking paler, and he started to worry she was pushing herself too hard.

Shaye pulled back with a gasp, Emma rushing over with a juice. "That was awful. Who hurts someone like that?" she asked, finishing the drink in a few swallows. "Her brain and skull are good now, if you want to work on stitching the wounds, Dad."

"I know you want to move to the other broken bones next, so let me set her shoulder first. Otherwise, it will jar her while you're working," he said. "Duncan, can you help hold her please?"

He could hear the shoulder popping back into place and was grateful Tess had put his mate to sleep. Once she was laid back down, Shaye placed her hand over her knee and her wrist. Her knee slowly started looking more like a knee, although it was still swollen. Her wrist no longer lay at an odd angle. Doc was working on some stitches along her scalp, Tess flushing the wounds as he went.

'Almost out,' Shaye said faintly. 'I got the bones, but I'll have to do the muscle repairs later. She definitely needs fluids and antibiotics. They beat her, multiple times, but that's it...spell...' her voice faded as she slumped forward. Ian rushed forward to catch her.

"We need a better chair that she won't fall out of," he grumbled.

"Or you guys could stop getting hurt," Doc countered.

"Bring her upstairs," Emma said. "I'll get food going for everyone."

"Just order pizza, dear. Everyone is tired," Doc said. He quickly washed his hands, laying one on Shaye's head.

"Is she okay?" Duncan asked.

Doc nodded. "Just used up all her energy. After she sleeps and gets a good meal, she'll be fine. She made a lot of good progress on Marge. I don't know that she would have made it another day," he said as Ian carried Shaye out of the room. Tess handed Doc a new set of sutures.

"What did she mean by 'that's it'?" Duncan asked.

Emma slipped from the room, but he could hear her in the kitchen.

"They didn't…uh…force…" Doc fumbled for words.

"Oh!" They didn't rape her, is what she meant. Thank god for small miracles.

He collapsed in the chair, holding his mate's hand as Doc and Tess worked around him. Her body still wasn't healing naturally and that worried him. With the major injuries out of the way, her natural shifter healing should have started in, even if it was slow due to lack of nourishment.

Tess ran her hands over Marge's body, hovering just above her. "The boy said they injected her with something?"

Duncan nodded. "He didn't know what it was though."

"Doc, do you see anything?" she asked.

"No, but I'm worried since the last thing Shaye said was spell. You already got the Tamer spell bracelet off."

"What if the injection was another spell?" Merri asked.

"Shit," Doc cursed.

Duncan heard the back door open, Berkley running in. "What is it?"

"What if the shot was a spell? I'm not seeing anything, but you're better at sensing spells. Can you take a look?"

"Wouldn't Shaye have fixed the spell first like she did with Sam?" Emma asked, back in the doorway.

"Not if it wasn't a death spell. She would have focused on healing the more life-threatening things first. She's a healer, not really a magic user like in spells. For Sam it was more using the magic of the mate and Clan bonds to destroy the spell. Her healing gift allowed her to see it, but she couldn't dismantle the magic herself. What she could do is focus all of us and show us where it was. Same for if this was a spell, she could see it, but she wouldn't have been able to fix it," Doc explained.

Berkley grunted, his face showing strain as he concentrated on Marge. "Gage!" he called out suddenly. "Look at this."

This room was suddenly getting crowded. Duncan looked at them anxiously. He couldn't sense anything, but then again magic wasn't really his thing.

"I've never seen something like this. They combined a Tamer spell with a suppression spell and made it injectable. No wonder she isn't healing. Between these two spells, she doesn't have a chance of reaching her shifter abilities," Gage said.

"What if we alter it here? Add a null here? Would that dismantle it?" Berkley asked.

Duncan had no idea what they were talking about.

Tess and Merri came closer. "Show us?" Tess asked.

Merri gasped. "I saw something like this. It was in an old book. I think it's at the library. I can go and find it and connect over the bond when I do. It's in the back room so I can't bring it here."

"Take Sam and Gawain with you," Rolf said. "I know we have the ward up over the town, but I still want to be careful."

They ran out of the room. The tension was high as they waited for them to make contact again.

"Where's the boy?" Duncan asked suddenly.

"He's right here," Emma replied, pointing behind the doorway. A head popped around the frame, cheeks full, cookie crumbs on his face.

'Here we go. This is the one I saw,' Merri suddenly said a few minutes later.

An image popped in Duncan's head showing a book lying open on a table.

"That does look similar," Berkley said. He grabbed a pad of paper and started writing it down.

Oh, yeah. Gage wouldn't have the Clan bond with them so he wouldn't be able to see it.

Gage studied it. "I think if we tweaked it a bit here, we could counter it," he said, pointing to a spot on the paper.

'Come back, Merri. It's better if we're all here to do the spell,' Berkley said.

Duncan was grateful the library wasn't far away. It only took a couple of minutes, he was sure they had been speeding the whole time, but the Sheriff clearly wasn't going to stop them. When Merri got back, she, Tess, Berkley, and Gage huddled around, exchanging ideas and wording. Duncan just held his mate's hand, letting their voices wash over him. He didn't understand a word they were saying.

"I think that's it," Gage said. "Doc, can you keep an eye on her while we work? I want to make sure there's no booby traps or backlash when we dismantle it."

It took them about forty-five minutes to slowly unravel the spell, and they all looked exhausted at the end. Emma had left a few minutes ago to get the pizza, the wolfdog following her. The boy stayed by the doorway, peeking in around the doorframe.

"It's gone," Berkley said, relief in his voice.

Emma came back to the room. "Food's ready," she said.

"She's stable for tonight. I'll change her IV before I go to bed," Doc said.

"I'll take the early morning change," Tess offered.

Duncan ate dinner and sat beside his mate all night long. The boy stayed with him, wanting to keep an eye on his friend. Rolf had pulled out two camping cots from the basement for them to use. It was going to be a restless night.

8

Marge woke up slowly, her entire body sore. But she was warm, the ground beneath her soft. She couldn't hear the drip of the water anymore. She tried to roll over, but a tug on her hand stopped her. Opening her eyes, she saw an IV sticking out of the top of her hand. Carefully moving her head, she looked around, seeing that she was in some sort of medical facility. It looked vaguely familiar. Her entire body sagged in relief when she realized she was in the Nightwood Clan house. This was Doc's room. They had found her. She felt a few tears escape. Marge had thought they would come for her, but after a couple of days she had started to give up hope. To know that they kept looking even with the scent blockers stopping them, meant everything.

'I'm glad you're awake,' a voice said softly.

Marge looked around and saw the boy. 'Are you okay?' she asked. He looked clean and he had all new clothes on, some sort of superhero pajamas.

He nodded. 'Your friends are nice. Miss Shaye helped fix my scratches and bruises this morning. Miss Emma gave me cookies last night and Sam even slipped me an extra one.' He grinned.

'I'm so glad. Was there a Sheriff here?' she asked. She wanted to know if Gage knew about the boy and could look into finding his parents.

'He was. He's a little scary, but he promised to try to find my parents.'

'Okay, now that I'm feeling better, tell me your name again. I can remember it now, I bet,' Marge said. She couldn't keep calling him "the boy."

'Jimmy,' he told her, grinning.

'Nice to meet you, Jimmy,' she said, smiling back at him.

'Did you know you have a mate?' he asked.

Marge startled. *'What?'*

'He found us yesterday. He's a really cool dragon. You should see how big he is! He's dark green with black marks all over him. It's really cool looking. They're making breakfast. It smells so good. I've been so hungry, and they keep giving me snacks and told me I can eat anything in the fridge I want. There's a couple really crunchy apples left, if you want one. We're going to make cookies later. Are you going to make cookies with us?' he asked, rambling happily.

Marge tried to process what was going on. The boy, sorry, Jimmy, was a chatterbox. He wasn't this chatty in the cave, although she couldn't say she had been very talkative or lively there either. He was warm, fed, and safe now, so he was probably comfortable enough to open up more. She tried to remember yesterday. There had been a roar and a surge of heat, she had grabbed the boy to try to protect him, and then nothing. She must have passed out. Looking around the room, she saw two cots folded up in the corner, but no one else was in the room.

'They didn't want you overwhelmed or crowded when you first woke up, so they're all waiting out in the kitchen and living room. He's right outside the door. I'm supposed to let him know when it's okay to come in.'

'He's nice?' Marge asked. It seemed so odd that everyone knew she had a mate but her. She tried to scent, but all she smelled was medical things. Of course, she didn't think Fate

would give her an awful mate, but then again, she never really expected to get a mate at all.

'Yup. I had a nightmare last night, but he didn't get mad when it woke him up. Just got me a glass of hot chocolate and sat with me. I'll go get him,' he said, running out of the room.

"You can go in now!" he said to someone outside the door before heading back toward the kitchen.

Marge's breath caught as a man stepped through the doorway. He was probably about six foot four, broad shoulders. He was dressed in a pair of worn jeans, the knees fraying. He had on a tight gray t-shirt, which showed off his flat stomach and delicious biceps. He had black tattoos covering his arms and she thought she could see more peeking out from his t-shirt. They were tribal looking, mostly geometric type of shapes with some swirls. Both his beard and his hair were black, his beard closely cropped. His gray eyes were so expressive, she could see worry and nervousness in them. He had a scar by his right eye, and she wondered how he got it.

"Hello," she said.

"Hi," he replied, hovering in the doorway. "Um, uh. I'm Duncan." Good grief, he sounded like an idiot, he thought to himself. He shifted on his feet unsure if he should come further into the room or wait until she invited him.

"I'm Marge. Which you probably know," she said, rolling her eyes at herself. "Can you come closer so I can scent you? I can't smell anything over the antiseptic."

He moved slowly into the room, not wanting to spook her cat. It was one of the reasons they let her wake up alone. The beast had been agitated, even in her sleep. After they had removed the Tamer/suppression spell, the cat had made itself known, shifting her hands into claws. They had needed to bring Gage in to calm her cat down, so she didn't fully shift. Doc had redone her IV once she had settled; although he had told Duncan that if there weren't any lingering signs of infection, he would take it out today.

Marge watched him come closer and she reached out a hand, grabbing his arm to pull him down so she could smell him. Oh, that smell. He smelled like the jungle, like wildness and a hint of campfire. He smelled like home. "Hello, mate," she said, staring into his eyes. She saw relief there when she claimed him.

"Hello," Duncan replied, raising her hand to kiss the palm. "Are you hungry? They're making a big breakfast."

"In a minute. Can you tell me what happened? I remember a roar and heat and then nothing." She watched as Duncan's cheeks flushed a light pink, sheepishness on his face.

"That was me. I kind of lost it when I saw you were hurt and may have let loose a little dragon fire."

"Did you get them all?" Marge asked, suddenly terrified they would come for her.

"Shh, mate. Shh," Duncan said soothingly as he bent down over her, an arm on either side.

She pulled him down as much as she could, turning her head to rest in the dip of his neck and shoulder. Breathing deeply, she let herself be surrounded by his scent.

"There were six there, five didn't, uh, make it. Marco came and took the sixth to get information out of him. He was injured. I haven't heard anything else about it. Ian checked the forest and there wasn't anyone else there," Duncan tried to reassure her. He could hear her heart racing. He wanted to run his fingers over her hair, but she still had stitches in, so he contented himself with holding her gently.

After several minutes, she forced herself to loosen her grip. She normally wasn't this clingy. "There was one more, the guy in charge. They never used names, so I just called him Boss Guy in my head. He wasn't there on the last day. Definitely some sort of paranormal, but they had blockers on the whole time, so I don't know exactly what he is."

"Gage said he was going to stop over later today if you

were up for it to talk about things. I have a feeling they think they know who it is," Duncan said.

There was a knock on the door and Marge looked over, seeing Doc in the doorway. "Do you mind if I check on you really quick? I can take the IV out if the infection is gone."

"Come in! Thank you for helping me," Marge said, her cat calm around Doc.

He gave her a smile before checking her stitches and closing his eyes. He kept one hand on her shoulder. "It looks like the infection is all gone, so let's get this IV out of you. I bet you'll be more comfortable. Your cuts look like they're pretty well healed as well. Do you want me to take the stitches out now, or wait until later?"

"Let's do it now. I can't wait to get a shower," she said.

Doc was incredibly gentle and soon enough all the stitches were removed, and she had a small bandage on her hand from where the IV had been pulled out. "That should stop bleeding soon, but your body is still working overtime. Shaye is going to finish up your healing session today, but let's get some food in you too. Breakfast should be ready in about ten minutes. I'm glad you're better," he said with a smile before leaving the room.

"Help me sit up?" she asked. She could tell a lot of her injuries were healed, but there was still some pain.

Duncan pressed the button on the bed, slowly moving it to a sitting position, watching Marge's face for signs of discomfort.

"Thank you. Now tell me the rest," she said. She sat there, amazed at how much she had missed. Duncan's voice was a little choked up when he described what her injuries had been.

"I knew whatever they shot me with wasn't good. It burned and I could feel it spreading throughout my body. I'm so glad the back room was kept safe. I'll have to get Merri her own key after this. I knew the wards would hold, but there's always a chance, right? Now tell me about you, please," she asked, wanting to know all about her mate. She had a feeling it would be another day or two before she felt up to creating the mating bond, but she wanted to be as close as possible to him.

"I'm a dragon, about eight hundred years old. Favorite color is green. I'm a sucker for poutine and chocolate cake. Not together, but those are my favorites," he laughed. "I have most of my things in storage since I haven't had a permanent home in a while. I was here last year, but only for a day to help them fight against Vlad. I had a dream where my sister told me to come back; I arrived just in time for the town meeting. I drive a motorcycle, although I think I'm going to need to get a truck living here. I like working with my hands. Lately I've been making sculptures. It's something I can do in either form. Oh! And I joined the Clan."

Wow. Okay. There were some things in there that they would need to explore later. She had a feeling his sister wasn't alive any longer. If she remembered the stories right, there was one dragon who had helped at the battle to avenge his sister.

"You joined the Clan?" she asked.

Duncan nodded. "I was already thinking these were good people and would be great friends. When I realized you were my mate, they were supportive and included me in all their plans. Tess said she had a dream where I was part of the Clan and Rolf offered me a place. I originally was going to think about it for a while; I'd been on my own for so long, it was an adjustment thinking that I would have this huge type of family if I joined. I was already leaning toward saying yes and then I finally caught your scent. I wanted to have the best support when it came to saving you, so I took the leap."

"Breakfast is ready!" Sam called out.

They both laughed. "He is not quiet," she said, cheered by the fact that some things never changed.

"Do you want me to grab you a plate?" Duncan asked.

"No. I want to eat out there. I just need some clothes," she said, just now realizing she was in her underwear underneath the blanket.

"Are you sure? I'm happy to bring it back." Duncan wasn't sure if she should move yet. Shaye still had a few things to heal, and while Marge's shifter healing was working again, it was a bit slow.

"Nope. I'm eating out there with the people who saved me," she said firmly.

Duncan nodded, knowing he had to let her be independent, even though he was feeling a little caveman-y and wanting to provide for her while she stayed here. "Emma brought down a robe earlier, if that would work?"

"Perfect," Marge replied. Duncan had to help her stand and put it on. She grunted as she tried to bend her knee.

"Shaye got the major injuries last night but passed out before she could get to the muscles. She was going to do it today after she woke up. Jimmy was up early, and she did a quick session on him, but your cat seemed agitated, and she didn't want to risk you shifting in your sleep and tearing out the stitches and the IV."

"I get it, I totally understand. Just stay by me so I don't fall?" she asked.

"Of course," Duncan replied, holding out an arm for her to take.

Marge made her way slowly to the kitchen, her mate hovering worriedly by her side. She was determined to eat with her friends this morning. It smelled delicious, pancakes or waffles maybe with bacon.

Sam was standing at the stove, a large griddle set up.

"Morning, Marge," Emma said. "Why don't you come sit down with me?" she asked, gently leading Marge over to sit at the kitchen table. It was close enough to the kitchen doorway that she could see in and feel like she was part of the family.

Shaye sat next to her, handing her a cup of tea. Her stomach was a little acidy, probably from the lack of food, and she was grateful Shaye had brought tea even though coffee was normally her drink of choice. They sat quietly for a few minutes before Shaye spoke again. Duncan kissed the top of her head before going into the kitchen to help with breakfast.

"I'm so glad you're here," Shaye said quietly.

Marge swallowed hard, her throat tightening. She took a sip of her tea, buying herself a minute before she responded. She had never been this emotional before. She blamed it on almost dying. Honestly, this group of people had done more for her than her own blood family ever had. Shaye had worked on her until she herself had passed out.

"Thank you for saving me," Marge replied, gently bumping her shoulder against Shaye's.

"Duncan did that. He's the one that found you," Shaye protested.

"Hmm. He told me how much it took out of you healing me," Marge said.

"If you're up to it, I can work on you again today. Once you were out of danger, your cat side seemed riled up and I didn't want to cause you any additional stress, so I wanted to wait until you were awake again," Shaye offered.

"I would appreciate that," Marge answered. She was touched that Shaye had read her so well. Her cat would have been on guard once the bracelet had been removed and she had been on the mend.

Shaye gave her a small smile, closing her eyes and taking Marge's free hand. Almost instantly, Marge felt a warmth flow through her body. Nothing hurt like she feared, but she could feel things mending, her strength coming back. She kept a close eye on Shaye, not wanting her to overexert herself again. Marge could always wait for another session.

She noticed Rolf standing in the doorway, watching. As a mate, it must be hard seeing your partner tire themselves out, even if you were proud of what they were doing.

Minutes later, when Shaye let go of her hand, Marge was amazed at how different she felt. She felt amazing. Duncan came in, bringing a plate of pancakes, a smile and a look of relief on his face when he saw her. She must be looking a lot better as well. Her stomach grumbled as she smelled the food. She hadn't felt hungry in days and it startled her.

Shaye laughed. "Well, I'm glad you're feeling better. They made plenty of food, so eat all you want." Rolf came over and handed Shaye a cup of coffee before heading back into the kitchen to bring more food out.

Marge was amazed. There were mounds of pancakes, sausage patties, muffins, and bacon.

"You'll have to tell me what you think of the pancakes," Sam said. "I'm trying out some of the huckleberries Merri and Gawain sent back from Montana."

"I don't know that I've ever had a huckleberry before," Marge said.

"I love them," Duncan said with a grin, glee in his voice. "I used to go berry picking when I lived in the mountains. It's been a while since I've had them."

Marge topped her pancakes with butter and a little bit of maple syrup before taking a bite. She moaned. The berries were juicy and flavorful. They were both sweet and a little tart, perfect for the pancakes.

Duncan bent down to whisper in her ear, his voice a little strangled. "Mate. Unless you want to go to the bedroom, you gotta stop making that noise."

Marge grinned up him. "Sorry, not sorry. These are so good. Maybe tomorrow?" she said, her eyes drinking him in. She could feel the other type of hunger coming back, Shaye having worked wonders.

Duncan swallowed hard, his dick hardening in his jeans.

"Tomorrow. Right. Sounds good. Great." He shifted in his seat, trying to relieve the pressure behind his zipper.

"Alright over there?" Sam asked, laughter in his voice, his eyes mischievous.

"Leave them alone," Tess said, smacking Sam in the chest.

"Thank you all for finding me," Marge said.

"You're one of us," Merri replied. "I'm so glad you're home."

9

Marge sat back, her stomach full. It had been a delicious breakfast and she felt normal again. She had kept an eye on Jimmy, who had eaten his weight in food. Emma's dog Rockefeller had taken a position right near his chair, hoping to catch some scraps. Merri saw him sneak the dog a few pieces of bacon and she was going to say something, but Emma had caught her eye and let her know it was okay.

They moved to the living room, Duncan bringing her another tea. Ian turned on some music, coming back to sit on the floor, nudging his way to sit between Berkley's legs. Emma sat in Doc's lap in another recliner, with the other mates scattered around the room sitting together. Her cat purred, content and safe. Family. These were her family, she thought. Although she may not have known them for very long, her cat seemed to have claimed them for itself. Her mate was already part of the Clan, so she would need to talk to Rolf at some point about joining herself. She still hadn't managed to get to every Sunday dinner, and now the prospect of joining the Clan felt huge. Going from a loner to a large family in such a short time would be a little bit of an adjustment.

The dog went on alert, staring at the front door. A knock sounded and Sam jumped up to answer it. Gage came through, holding a book.

"Morning," he said.

"Did you eat already? We have some leftovers," Emma offered.

"Thank you, but I already ate," he said, smiling at Emma. He looked over at Marge and she could see the relief in his face. "I'm glad to see you looking better, old friend."

"I'm not that old," she grumbled back, falling into their routine. His grin lit up his face, one he normally didn't show to most people. He must be comfortable around Rolf's group as well.

"I had some things to go over if you're willing. I know it was only yesterday that we got you back, but the quicker we move, the better chance we have of finding these guys," he said, an apology in his tone.

She felt Duncan shift next to her, but he didn't say anything. "I'll tell you what I can."

"Me too," Jimmy piped up. "Did you find my parents yet?"

"Not yet. I think I have it narrowed down to a certain region though," Gage replied. Marge wasn't sure what to make of that look on his face. She would ask him later when the boy wasn't around.

"What about Barry? Did you find him, or did he bribe you to hide him too?" he asked angrily.

There was a collective gasp in the room at the name. Marge felt the boy's power leak out.

"That's enough!" she said firmly. "We do not use our power on our friends. Gage would never do that and if he did, the house wards would never have let him in." She did find it odd that Gage didn't answer the boy right away, but then again, she didn't know the limits of his magic and shifter side. There were rumors of a few people being immune even to TruthSpeak.

"Plus, the town's wards would have kicked him out," Berkley added.

"Town wards?" Marge asked, distracted.

Duncan sighed. "I knew I forgot something. They cast a protective ward that covers all of the town, even the outskirts. No one who means harm can enter, and if they were already here, the wards push them out. Hey, is Steve still here?" he asked, curious.

"Steve? What about Steve?" Marge felt like she was missing something.

"I called a town meeting. We didn't feel right enacting the spell without letting the town know what was going on. Steve wasn't the biggest fan of finding out paranormals are real," Gage said.

"He's all talk and hot air, from what I've seen. He has a short temper, and his mouth sometimes runs, but he doesn't actually cause any harm," Marge said. Steve was a frequent visitor to the library. She thought he didn't have many friends in town and came to the library to be near other people. He was often grumpy, and she wondered if he still had lingering pain after his accident.

"He's still here," Gage said. "He's avoiding some of us that he knows are paranormals, but he hasn't said anything else. Now, Marge is right. We do not use our gifts on friends to force them to answer," he said. Marge thought his tone was just right, firm and laced with disappointment, but not angry.

"Whoever was with your kidnappers used a blocker the entire time. I had Marco come in as well, and while there is something familiar there, we can't put a face or a name to it. Marge, did they use any names?"

She shook her head. "There was one time someone started to say something with a B and was hit, but when someone else addressed him as Boss, I thought that had been what he was going to say. I would recognize them, but I don't have a name."

"It's Barry," the boy protested. "Why don't you believe me?"

Gage crouched down in front of him. "I do believe you, but I need lots of proof if I'm going to go after him. He's powerful and I can't just go accusing him without proof, real solid, can't ignore proof. I have lots of stories and things he may be linked to, but he's careful not to leave evidence of himself behind."

Standing back up, he handed some photos to Marge. "Can you look through these and see if you see anyone you recognize?"

Marge flipped through, listening as Gage updated everyone on what he had been doing. It seemed like he was still getting reports of those flyers coming in from other Wardens.

"This one!" she yelled. "This is the boss guy. The tall one behind him was Minion One." It was a group photo at some event, but she pointed out each one. Gage pulled out the book, opening it to a page before handing it to her. "Bartholomew, Barry, Jones," she read. "Convocation member. Crap. How do we fight against a Convocation member?"

There was a pop of air and Marco was suddenly standing there. She had met him a few times over the years when he had visited Gage.

"Lots of evidence. I just got done with the guy from the cave. Recorded the whole thing. He was Barry's assistant and was quite aware of what Barry was up to. He told me where to look to find some records that supported his claims. Barry's been supplying human hunters the blockers and paranormal detectors like the one Ian and Berkley ran into in Scotland. From what he said, Barry's behind the whole resurgence of hunters. He was going to say something else, but there must have been a spell I didn't detect that activated and killed him."

"What was he saying?" Rolf asked.

"Something about 'he's keeping' and then he died," Marco replied.

"We came across a different type of thing with Marge as well. They made a combination Tamer and suppression spell and used it as an injectable. We didn't sense it at all until Shaye caught it. Maybe he had a sleeper spell on him," Doc suggested.

"Did anyone check Jimmy for a spell?" Marge asked, worried Barry had installed one on the kid.

Shaye nodded. "I looked when I healed him this morning and didn't find anything. Berkley also looked."

"Jimmy, how long were you with Barry?" Gage asked.

"Two years," he replied.

"How did he get you?"

Jimmy told the same story he had told Marge. Fake policeman came to his school and took him.

"If the police came to the school, there should be some record. Everyone has to be signed out if they left early," Shaye said. "Even if they used fake names, there should be a signature, maybe even video in the police evidence."

Gage shook his head. "I already checked. There was a sign-out that day, but it didn't lead anywhere. There was no police report filed."

"There was no missing persons?" Tess asked softly. Marge understood. If his parents didn't file a missing persons report with the human or paranormal authorities, did that mean they were in cahoots with Barry or were they dead?

"Did Barry bring you anywhere?" Gage asked Jimmy.

"Sometimes. Never around a lot of people. Sometimes he had prisoners and he made me talk to them and ask them questions. There were a couple other Convocation members that came around a lot," Jimmy replied.

"Can you find them in this book and circle them for me?" Gage asked.

Emma stood up. "Why don't you come in the kitchen and get a quick snack first? It's been a little bit since breakfast."

After they left the room, Ian asked quietly, "Are you thinking his parents are dead or gave him to Barry?"

"I'm leaning toward they actively were working with Barry in some way. There's no missing child report that matches his description, especially where he said he grew up. Marco popped over and talked to the neighbors. It seems the parents moved away about the same time frame, but people don't really remember seeing the kid with them. The school secretary who let him go has signs of having her memories altered. If she tried to stop them or asked questions, they would have had to do something to get the boy. She would have been too hard to kill as it would have brought in human authorities, so I think they used a spell or compulsion on her. Until we know for sure though, I'm going to keep it quiet. I don't want someone claiming him just to give him back to Barry. Can he stay with you?" Gage asked quietly.

"I'll take him," Marge found herself volunteering. She and the boy had bonded in the cave. She saw Duncan nodding and realized she probably should have talked to her mate first.

Berkley left the room but came back a few minutes later. "I made these this morning. There's one for each of you. They'll glow when there's danger nearby. No one else but us would be able to see it. They'll also conceal your paranormal status from human hunters. With Convocation members involved, we thought it would look too suspicious if it hid us from other paranormals. If we ran into Barry or the other two Convocation members, there's a chance they would know we were supposed to be paranormals since we had to file Clan paperwork. They already know Marge is a paranormal as well. They'll still alert to any danger, including paranormal and will protect against evil intentions. They'll also adjust to your shifted size, so don't take them off," he said, handing them each a pendant.

"How much protection?" Duncan asked.

"Mostly spells and mind attacks. I'm working on a physical protection spell as well, but the wording gets a little more complicated," Berkley replied.

"Thank you," Marge said, sliding hers on. "How's the library? They knocked me out before leaving, so I didn't get to see if they did any more damage."

"We've got a new computer monitor coming," Merri said. "The tower was fine. Everything else has been cleaned up and replaced if it was broken. We told the town that the library was closed until further notice. They also all know you were kidnapped, so you may be mobbed when you come back."

Jimmy and Emma rejoined them in the living room, cookie crumbs around the corners of his mouth. "I found them," he said, handing the book back to Gage.

"Can you sneak into their office and see what you can find?" Gage asked Marco.

"Yup."

"Hold on, Marco," Emma said, hurrying out of the room. She came back with a bag of cookies. "Here, so you don't get hungry," she said.

"Thank you," he replied, giving her a brief rare smile before disappearing.

10

Marge felt…needy. Horny. She was regretting the fact that she had said she wanted to wait to bond. She had thought she would take longer to heal, but Shaye's healing had been incredible. She had gone to bed early last night, a little tired since her body was still catching up on some blood loss. Her mate had chosen to sleep in another room to give her space, but now she was going to hunt him down. Her cat side was ready to claim its mate and so was she.

She threw open her door but caught it before it banged into the wall. She didn't want to damage Rolf's house or wake anyone up. It was pretty early. She gently shut her door, but she only made it a few feet before a door opened. Ian walked out of his room, giving her a glimpse of Berkley still sprawled across the sheets.

"Hey, Marge. I was just going to get the coffee going. Did ye need anything?"

She shook her head.

"Ah. If you're looking for tall, dark-haired, and winged, he's on the left, first door on the other side of the stairs.

Dinnae worry; the walls are weel insulated and pretty sound-proof," he teased before loping down the stairs.

Marge smiled and continued hunting her mate. She would have found him by his scent, but at least now she didn't have to sniff every door. She knocked softly, because it was the polite thing to do, but didn't hear any answer. Cracking the door open a smidge, she heard soft snores from the bed. Strolling in, she admired her mate. He was naked, at least from the waist up, sleeping on his stomach, his body smooth with little hair. His ass was nicely rounded, but the sheet was covering it, his toes sticking out at the bottom. He either hated having the sheet tucked in or was a restless sleeper. His back was nicely sculpted, the muscles showing even in rest. His arms were tucked under the pillow. His biceps looked incredibly strong, and she wondered if she would be able to simply hang from them for a while. The black hair was cut close on the sides, but the top was a little longer; long enough that it gave her something to hold on to or run her fingers through. His eyes were framed by incredibly long lashes. The skin on his arms, thighs, and back was covered in black markings. She couldn't wait to trace each one.

"Are you going to stand there all day, mate?" a sleep-roughened voice asked. Moving her eyes back to his face, she saw his eyes were open and he had a smirk on his face.

"Depends on if you're open to completing our mating this morning or if I need to come back later," she said, sassing him back.

She let out a little scream as he moved faster than she thought possible to grab her and toss her on the bed.

"I am more than ready to claim you, mate. I only wanted to make sure you were fully healed first and were ready," Duncan replied, crouching over her.

Marge's eyes skimmed the rest of his body, moaning when she realized he had slept naked, and he was already hard. His cock was long, probably nine or ten inches, and thick. She reached out, running her fingertips over the shaft, drifting down to tease his sac. Marge grinned as she felt a little shiver run through him. He moved to lie next to her, a leg thrown over hers, his hand coming up to cup her breast, thumb gently rubbing the nipple.

"I'm so glad I found you," he said quietly.

"Me too," she replied, turning on her side to give him a soft kiss to his lips, her hands playing in his hair. His beard tickled a little; she wasn't used to kissing someone with facial hair. His lips parted, giving her tongue access to kiss him deeper, her tongue twining around his. The kiss quickly turned out of control, igniting both of their desires, their hands groping and touching any part of each other they could reach. She loved staring into his gray eyes, seeing lust and desire in them. She had never felt sexier.

Grabbing her hips, Duncan rolled, ending up with her sitting on top of him, his cock riding along her back end. Reaching up, he cupped her breasts, his fingers playing with her nipples, encouraging them to harden. Once they were pointed, he sat up, sticking a tongue out to lick them, gently sucking one into his mouth through the fabric of her shirt, his hands around her waist. Marge grabbed his hair, pulling his head back so she could kiss him again. The man was an amazing kisser, she could sit here all day kissing him. She reached one hand behind her, slowly stroking his shaft, feeling the drips of precum easing the way. She took a deep breath, drawing in his essence, her vagina getting wet. Duncan drew in his own breath, trailing one hand across her hip to tease along her folds.

"You're wearing too many clothes," he muttered, shifting his hand to his dragon claws, cutting away her pajamas.

"Good thing those weren't my favorite." She looked at him, eyebrow quirked.

"Needed to see you," he replied, licking his lips at the sight of her breasts. Her nipples were still hard from his playing with them. He cupped them again, bringing her breasts closer to his mouth, licking around the areola gently, swirling his way to the nipple.

She moaned as his mouth closed around her, his teeth gently nibbling. She spread her legs farther to the sides, encouraging him to touch her core. She was wet and needy, wanting his touch. Duncan slid one hand slowly down her side, a finger brushing across her pubis. She kept it closely trimmed, but she had a strip of hair on her mons. He teased her, playing with the curls before barely glancing over her clitoris. Marge grabbed his head, forcing him to look at her.

"More, now. Please," she demanded.

Duncan smiled, her nipple between his front teeth. He applied a little more pressure, still just barely glancing over her bud. Marge rocked her hips, desperate to get some friction. Duncan kept his finger still, letting her ride his hand. He raised his knees, placing his feet flat on the bed. With a gentle push, he encouraged her to recline, letting his legs support her. As she leaned back, his thumb landed on her clit, applying pressure while his other hand slid between her folds. He didn't have much room to work, but he thrust a finger into her heat, his thumb rubbing over her clit.

"I need more," she whimpered, her skin felt tight, extra sensitive. She was so close, but it wasn't enough.

Duncan slid two more fingers in, stretching her to take his girth before he lifted her up and slid her down over his shaft. Marge hissed at the small bite of pain from his width despite the stretching, but she loved how full he made her feel. Leaning forward, she took his mouth in a kiss, her tongue exploring his mouth as her hips started to ride him. Duncan let her set the pace, one hand gripping her hip, the other fondling her breasts. He felt so good inside her, warm and hard, smooth and thick. She was so full. As her hips rose and fell, she knew they wouldn't last long this first time, the excitement of claiming their mate would push them to complete the bond soon. Her legs began to tire, but Duncan grabbed her by the hips keeping her steady as he started to thrust into her, his shaft dragging across nerve endings, pulling almost all the way out before slamming back in. He adjusted her angle just a smidge with his legs and she screamed as her orgasm ripped through her as he hit her G-spot.

"I take you, Duncan, as my Mate. To love and cherish forevermore," Marge gasped out, shifting her hand to her claws to rake at Duncan's chest. He now had her marks starting at his collarbone arching toward his left nipple.

Duncan gripped her tightly, thrusting a few more times before grunting out, "I take you, Marge, as my Mate. To love and cherish forevermore." His hand changed to his talons and cut a mark at the curve where her neck and shoulder met. He blew a hot breath over the cut, and her skin tingled like she had a sunburn. She felt the heat of his climax inside her, a smile breaking over her face as she felt their bond solidify. After being alone for so many years, she now had a mate, friends, and what could be her family if she let them.

Marge collapsed on top of Duncan's chest, both of them breathing heavily, their skin slightly sweaty. They probably needed a shower, but she didn't want to move. Eventually, she rolled against his side, snuggling in with her head on his shoulder, her arm resting across his chest. After a few minutes, she lifted her head to study his body.

"Are these tattoos?" she asked, tracing the black lines on his skin.

"No. They appeared when I shifted the first time," Duncan replied. "I never had them before I shifted and they were on my dragon form. I'm not sure why I have so many; never got a good answer out of anyone."

"I like them," Marge said, kissing one of the swirls closest to her.

"I'm glad. Sometimes I get weird looks or people avoid

me. I'm tall, not exactly weak looking, covered in what looks like tats, and I ride a motorcycle. You have one now too, from the mate mark. It won't affect your job at all, will it?"

Marge shook her head. "No. I'm Guardian of the Library. As far as the town knows, it's a public library, but since it also houses a paranormal one, it's more of a privately owned library. It's handed down to each Guardian, deed to the land, everything. It's a way to protect the paranormal side from ever accidently being sold or destroyed. Not that they would be able to destroy the wards on mine, but not everyone is lucky enough to have this level of protection."

"Well, you'll be able to be Guardian for a long, long time then," Duncan said. "Dragons live quite a while."

"I never did figure out if dragons are immortal or not. There's not much information available."

"Hmm… Not a true immortality. Kind of like the Fae. We can be killed, it's just really hard to do it. In dragon form, our scales act as armor, protecting us from pretty much every-thing. Now, I haven't gone playing with some of the newer weapons like tanks and the bigger bombs, but I did survive a grenade accidentally going off."

Marge surged up to reach his lips, giving him a kiss. "No more playing with things that might kill you. How did you even get near a grenade?"

"I think I told you I build sculptures?" Duncan asked.

When Marge nodded, he continued. "I like to reuse things as much as possible and collect scrap metal. Someone dropped off a bunch of junk metal and it was in the box. They probably thought it was a dud, but it was still live and did not like my dragon fire when I tried to melt it."

"What kind of sculptures do you make?" Marge asked, curious.

"Mostly big ones." He grinned. "I make a lot of them in dragon form, so they're about as tall as a person, sometimes larger. I do make smaller ones as well, but I have a lot of fun making the big ones. I'll have to find a new place to create that won't be too obvious when I'm in my dragon form."

"I bet Rolf will let you do it here. Ian and Berkley just built a workshop on the grounds," she replied.

"I can ask him. I would need something, even if it's a simple structure made from cinderblocks to keep the flames away from the forest. I wouldn't want to accidently catch anything on fire," he said. "If not, I can try to find something that might work by the town. I'd like to keep it in the town limits so it would be under the new wards. Then you can come visit and it would be safe."

"I'd love to see what you make," Marge said, giving him a kiss.

"Do you want to play a game?" Duncan asked.

Merri wasn't sure if she should trust the look in his eyes. "What game? We just played Hide the Sausage."

Duncan barked out a laugh. "No! Not that kind of game, although that one was delightful. I have a hidden design somewhere on my body."

"Really?" Marge asked, sitting up excitedly. "Let me see!"

"You have to find it," Duncan replied laughing, "or it's not a game."

Marge started on his thighs, looking them over closely, trying her best to ignore his cock. It all looked like tribal tats and swirls to her. Moving up his body, she used her fingers to trace the markings, hoping it would jump out at her.

Duncan squirmed underneath her. "Are you ticklish?" she asked with a grin.

"Hmm. Nope. Not ticklish. Not me. I'm a big bad dragon. We don't get ticklish," he replied, biting his lip and clenching the covers as she skimmed over his hipbones.

"Uh huh. We'll see. I'm coming back as soon as I find this design," Marge threatened.

Marge searched, but other than having some fun biting his

nipples, she didn't see anything that stood out. "Flip over," she ordered.

'Bossy mate,' Duncan said over their new telepathic link.

'I can't believe I forgot to try this!' Marge said, excited. She leaned forward and pressed a kiss between his shoulder blades. Her eyes slightly crossed, and she let out a little scream.

"I found it," she shouted.

"Ow! That's my eardrum I think you just ruptured," Duncan replied, rubbing the injured appendage.

"I did not. It's wings! I see a little set of wings. They're buried beneath all the other markings though. I never would have noticed them if you didn't have me look."

"Every dragon has one hidden somewhere on their body, always someplace where it wouldn't be easily seen. Even if it's hot I normally have a t-shirt or tank top on, or a swim shirt if I'm in the water."

"Is it always on the back?"

"Nope. There was one guy I knew back when we were kids who claimed his was on his butt cheek," he answered.

There was a knock on the door.

"Apparently breakfast is ready," Duncan said.

"How do you know?"

"Um, when I joined the Clan, it came with a telepathic link with everyone."

"I've never heard of that before except for the old blood-bonds..." she trailed off, looking at him incredulously.

"Yeah," he said, drawing out the word. "I wanted the best resources available when it came to finding you. They formed the Clan the usual way, but in order to save Sam, they ended up doing a blood-bond pledge."

"Merri never said anything," Marge huffed. "I am totally going to pick her brain."

"I don't think anyone outside of the Clan knows. Gage, but definitely no one else. They didn't want the Convocation to know just how different this Clan was," Duncan said, a warning in his voice.

"I get it. I heard what they were worried about before, and now that we know Barry is part of these hunters, their fears are justified. I'll have to talk to Rolf about joining too."

"I'm sure they'd love that. They were all extremely worried about you. I think you have more family than you know. Let's grab a shower and head down to breakfast," Duncan said, lifting her off the bed and carrying her to the bathroom.

As they entered the room, she eagerly looked at her mate mark; the cut from his talon already starting to heal, with a pair of black wings tattooed over the top.

11

Marge lay in the hammock, enjoying the lazy breeze. She decided to give herself one more day off before going back to the library. She wasn't quite ready to face all the attention that might happen when the townspeople realized she was back. Jimmy was curled up in a chair, reading a book. He had settled in a lot faster than she had expected. He seemed to be loving the chance to be a little boy instead of being forced to use his magic for evil purposes. Well, she assumed they were evil purposes. Nothing Barry had done so far had been even close to reasonable, so her guess was that Jimmy had seen a lot of situations like hers and most of them probably hadn't ended well.

Today was grill-out day and the guys were busy getting everything ready. Tess and Emma were making pretzel rolls to go with dinner, Shaye was making a couple types of cookies for dessert. Even Gage said he was going to stop over as long as nothing popped up. The great thing about the ward was that it seemed to have cut down on even petty crimes.

Gage was still looking into Jimmy's parents, but it wasn't looking good. They seemed to have disappeared; credit cards stopped being used, bank accounts emptied, no parking tickets, no bills of any sort. With nothing else to go on, Marco would probably need to scent trace them. The house had still had a faint enough trace of their scent. They wanted to make absolutely sure where the boy's parents stood. They didn't want to take a chance that Barry could get his hands on him again. Emma had found some homeschooling materials online and had restarted the boy's education. Barry had kept him out of school for the two years he had had him, so he was too far behind to go to regular school at the moment. He was a quick learner though and they were going to do their best to get him caught up. Gage came over a few times to teach him how to control his magic better so he wouldn't accidentally use his TruthSpeak gift on someone, especially when he was out in town. They hadn't left the Clan's estate, not knowing what to say if anyone asked about him. Maybe she could say he was her nephew staying for a visit.

Marge was worried that his parents wouldn't be able to take him back or that they would find out for sure they were working with Barry. She didn't want him to just go into a foster care system and get lost or misunderstood. He had nightmares from his time with Barry, although he claimed they were better since he was here.

'You know we're going to adopt him, if that's the case. I already brought it up to Gage. He has someone who can create the paperwork for us, if we need it,' Duncan told her. He was inside drawing up a plan and researching materials for his workshop. Rolf had looked so pleased when Duncan had asked him. *'Jimmy will be fine. He's being adopted into this crazy family.'*

Marge smiled. It was true. Emma baked cookies with him, the guys would take him into the woods and run with him on the trails, teaching him things about nature. Merri brought him books from the library, Shaye and Tess had gone shopping and bought him a bunch of clothes and a phone that had all their numbers already programed in. He had been a big fan of Sunday family dinners and game night. Marge was eager to participate in the Inebriated Inconsistencies night that they sometimes had. It was a drinking game to documentaries; every time the show got something wrong, you had to drink. Maybe they could include Jimmy by giving him hot chocolate.

'I think I have the basics down for the workshop,' Duncan said. *'What do you think? Rolf said there will already be a gas line, if I wanted to work on smaller pieces in my human form as well. It's nothing fancy but there will be enough room to store a few pieces.'*

Marge looked at the images Duncan sent over their link. *'I like it. Will there be a bathroom or are you just going to pee in the woods?'* she joked.

'I can probably tap into the plumbing for Ian and Berkley's workshop. Rolf's going to get some contractors out to look at it. They were the ones who installed the workshop, so they'll know where everything is.'

'When Jimmy's ready and it's safe, we should bring him to see the paranormal museum. I think he would get a kick out of it. Merri and Gawain have been so excited to get it together. They were trying to decide when to have the grand opening, but the town's wards might actually help with that. It will give them peace of mind of who can enter into the museum, although they already had a lot of protections on it,' Marge said. She really thought the boy would like to look at all the items. But it would need to wait until they figured out his parent situation.

Speaking of, he had been awfully quiet the last few minutes. Marge looked over, finding him curled up in the chair, book fallen to the seat, fast asleep. *'He's out. I'm going to carry him inside to bed. Don't want him to get sunburned.'*

She quietly made her way over to him, letting him get her scent before she laid the book on his stomach and picking him up. He would get to a healthy weight while living here, but she thought he was still a little underweight for his age and height. If what she witnessed in the cave was an indication of how he was normally treated, he hadn't been getting anywhere near enough calories. He snuggled in, not waking all the way. Duncan met her at the porch holding the back door open and following her up the stairs. The boy had been given the room right next to Duncan to keep him close to them. Marge bent down, laying him gently on the bed before pulling the blanket off the floor to cover him.

'He's getting close to shifting age. We'll have to keep an eye on it,' she said. While they knew he was a paranormal, his scent wasn't strong enough to tell them exactly what kind he was, other than some sort of water-based shifter. He said he couldn't remember his parents talking about it or shifting in front of him. Which just seemed weird to her. Even her own mother, who had ditched her as soon as she could reasonably fend for herself, had taught her what kind of shifter she was and about their background. Based on the look on everyone's faces, it also seemed weird to them. She wasn't holding on to much hope that his parents were going to turn out to be reasonable people. There were enough red flags in the things they had learned about his life before them.

'What are we going to do if he's some sort of salt-water-based shifter?' Marge asked.

'Ask Rolf to put in a salt-water pool,' Duncan replied.

Marge looked at her mate, trying to figure out if he was serious. *'Seriously. We had this talk too. He and Ian think he's going to be something fresh-water based on his scent, something about salt-water shifters having a slight scent of the ocean to them, which he doesn't have. But he said if it turns out they were wrong, he offered to install a salt-water pool. Everyone would enjoy it and it would be good for his shifter side. We can take a vacation every year to the ocean. We'll figure it out and now we have a Clan that can help,'* Duncan replied, leading her from the room. Like all of the bedrooms, this one had blackout curtains, but they had bought a nightlight for him to try to help with the nightmares. After making sure it was on, she followed Duncan out of the room.

"Did you have any plans for the rest of the day?" Duncan asked.

"No. I was just enjoying the sunshine. I didn't want to go back to work yet," she replied.

"I haven't met your cat yet. I was wondering if you wanted to go running through the woods or maybe I could take you flying?" Duncan asked, looking at her hopefully.

Marge startled. She hadn't realized that she hadn't fully shifted since she had been taken. She supposed she had met his dragon, but she had been unconscious, so she wasn't sure it really counted on her end. His dragon would be familiar with her scent though.

"Let's go outside and I can shift, then I want to go flying," Marge said as they walked down the stairs. "It's still daylight though, should we wait to fly until tonight?"

Duncan hummed. "The townspeople already know about us, and I took off in the daytime once I scented you at the library, so they may have seen me already. I don't want to take off from here and give away the location if hunters are watching the town though. If anyone went back to the woods to get you or Jimmy, they would have scented me. Plus, the burned ground would have been a big clue a dragon had been there. Maybe we should wait until tonight," Duncan said, sounding disappointed.

As they walked through the kitchen to get to the back door, Berkley called out.

"Duncan, Marge, hold up!" He ran up to them from the library. "Sorry, I meant to grab you last night and forgot. Duncan, can I have your pendant for a minute? I realized I forgot to add a concealment spell on yours. That way if you go flying, you won't be spotted."

"Will it hide Marge as well? I wanted to take her flying today," Duncan asked curiously.

"Is she going to be riding you or are you holding her? If you're holding her, it should conceal her. I can try to word it so it will conceal her if she's riding you, but it would be a general spell that would conceal anyone who was on you. At least until I can figure out how to word it a little more specifically."

"I can ride in your claws for now," Marge said. She wasn't quite sure about riding on Duncan's back until they practiced, and she figured out how to hold on when they were hundreds of feet up in the air.

'I wouldn't let you fall,' Duncan told her, amusement in his voice.

'Logically, I know that. We'll just have to practice a little bit before I try riding on your back or something.'

"So just the concealment spell for your dragon?" Berkley asked, holding Duncan's pendant in the palm of his hand.

Duncan nodded and they watched as Berkley covered the pendant with his other hand. It took less than a minute before they saw a flash of light and Berkley handed the necklace back. "That should do it. The Clan will still be able to see you, but others won't," Berkley said.

"Thanks. Hey, Jimmy is sleeping. Can you keep an ear out for him? I don't think we'll be gone too long, but if you hear him can you let him know we're coming back?" Marge asked.

"Of course. It's been nice having him here. Have fun," he said before heading out of the kitchen.

Duncan grinned, almost vibrating with excitement. "Ready? I want to meet your cat."

Marge smiled back and led the way out to the backyard. She moved over to the side of the house so she wouldn't be easily seen from the library or kitchen windows. She pulled off her clothes, placing them on a bench that had been placed there for that purpose. Duncan watched as she crouched down, her body contorting to her cat form. It didn't take long; she had always been a fast shifter, and she was glad to see that the Tamer bracelet and spell didn't have any lingering side effects.

She stretched, loosening her muscles, getting ready for a quick pounce on her mate. She could scent him even stronger now and he smelled delicious. Looking around, she saw he was squatting down a few feet away watching her.

"You're gorgeous," Duncan said softly.

Marge sat down, licking her paw, preening a bit. She watched him closely, but it didn't look like he was going to come closer. She bunched her leg muscles, shifting subtly, getting ready to pounce on her mate. She jumped, keeping her claws in so she wouldn't accidently harm him, her front paws landing on his shoulders knocking him backward. Following, she landed on top of him, her paws gently kneading his chest, her chest rumbling with chuffs. Duncan's hands came up, gripping her head, staring into her eyes.

"Hey there mate. It's nice to meet your cat. I can't wait to go running with you one day. There's a cool stream at the back of the property I think we can have fun at. Maybe you could fish. I love the rosettes in your fur. You kind of have to be close to see them, don't you," Duncan said, running a hand down her fur.

Marge rumbled an agreement, eager to see his dragon and go flying. She gave him a kiss.

"Did you just lick me?" Duncan asked incredulously. "You have a rough tongue."

Marge nodded. She did. It helped with eating in this form. She had been gentle though so she wouldn't hurt his face. Scooting backwards, she ran back to her clothes, shifting quickly and throwing on her clothes.

"Okay, let's go. I want to fly," she said eagerly.

Duncan laughed. "Alright, back up a bit. I take up a bit more space when I'm a dragon," he said with a grin.

Marge moved back to the bench, watching as he shifted. He definitely took up more space in this form. She would guess he was the size of a small house if he curled up. If he laid out, tip of tail to snout, she would guess he would be the length of five or six minivans. He was huge. His wingspan was equally impressive as he shook them out. His body was a deep emerald green, the black markings showing up in this form as well. Even his wings had markings, although they were more subtle against the darker skin. The underside of his neck, where most beings were more vulnerable had over-lapping plates, reminding her a bit of the underside of a snake. His head was covered in flared spikes, including two jutting slender black horns. The spikes flowed down the back of his neck, almost like a mane. At least she would have something to hold on to if she ever rode on his back, she reasoned. His eyes were still gray, but now had slitted pupils, just like she did in her cat form. Duncan let out a tiny roar, letting her see all the sharp teeth in his mouth. They were going to have so much fun hunting together.

He waited for her to approach him. "You're amazing. I love your colors. I can even see green in my shifted form." She ran her hand over his leg, surprised at how warm he was. "I won't be cold with you, will I? You're so warm." She walked around him, taking in all his features, learning this side of her mate, his wings still spread giving her shade from the sun. As she reached his front again, he opened his hand, or well, paw. Talons? Claws? She wasn't sure what they were called. Placing his hand on the ground, backside down, fingers open, he had her climb into his hand before gently closing the talons around her. She was held safely, but she could still see through his fingers.

'*Ready?*' he asked.

'*Ready!*' she replied excitedly. His wings started to beat, pulling his body upward and soon they were higher than the treetops.

12

'*Hold on,*' he said, giving her a minute before pulling up sharply, his wings dragging through the air, keeping them afloat. Marge laughed, grabbing onto one talon as much as she could. He tightened his hold a bit, so she didn't tumble around inside his hand. As soon as they leveled off, he loosened his grip again, giving her enough space to see out but not fall through his fingers. It was like being in an airplane, she thought as he took her over the part of the forest that was in the ward. She saw some movement and he gently dove down, showing a bear climbing through the trees looking for berries. His body banked to the left and they flew by a waterfall, close enough she could feel the mist. The forest was green, dotted with a few patches of wildflowers. There were creeks, waterfalls. It was beautiful. She never would have seen this without Duncan. Marge held on as his body turned to the left again, following the edges of the ward, careful not to pass through them. They headed toward town, and she could see the top of her library. Everything looked good from up here.

Duncan brought them down lower, skimming over the

buildings. He was mostly gliding at this point, using the wind currents like a bird.

"Oh shit!" Marge suddenly shouted.

'What?' he asked sharply, looking around for hunters or other dangers.

'I think that's Marshall,' she said, pointing to a dark spot in the road up ahead.

'What in the world is he doing in the middle of the road?' Duncan asked.

'I don't know. He's never done that before,' Marge responded. She had known him for years and he was always careful about where he shifted. He was a large tortoise, so not native to the area, but there were a few found throughout the state. Generally, it turned out to be ones people bought as pets and later released into the wild. *'He's going to get hit if that car doesn't stop,'* she said, panicking, seeing a car driving toward the unaware shifter. She didn't want to watch poor Marshall go splat.

Duncan tried to speed up, but the width of the street prohibited him from fully opening his wings. He tried to squeeze between the buildings as much as possible so he could grab the shifter out of the way of the oncoming car but had to swerve up when a truck pulled out in front of him. He watched in horror as the car came closer and knew he wouldn't make it in time.

Marge squirmed, thinking maybe she could drop down and pull him out of the way. Suddenly a man ran out in front of the car, arms spread. Brakes screeched as the driver slammed on the brakes, coming to a sudden stop.

"What the hell, man?" the driver shouted out the window.

"Look where you're going, asshole! You almost ran over the turtle," the savior replied.

Duncan knew that voice from somewhere, but the man's back was toward them.

"It's just a turtle," the man in the car replied.

"Well, let me run over your pet rabbit then, Paul. It's just a rabbit. There's plenty more of them," the turtle saver replied sarcastically.

"Don't be such a dick, Steve. Get it out of my way."

"Slow the fuck down. Maybe if you weren't speeding and looking at your phone you would have seen it. What if it had been a person?"

Duncan was flabbergasted. Steve? The dick from the town meeting had put his life in danger to save what he thought was a simple turtle? What was going on? He perched on top of the building next to them, opening his talons further so Marge could see the drama better.

"Come on, turtle. You got to get out of the road. I've got some very nice greens in my yard, and I'll get you some water. You must be thirsty," Steve said, trying to walk backwards and cajoling the tortoise into following him. Marshall, if that was him, followed Steve easily and it looked like eagerly.

'Is this freaking you out as well? Or is it just me? I feel like we fell into an alternate universe where Steve is nice.'

'He's not that bad,' Marge protested. 'He's a bit of a loud mouth and he doesn't like change, but he's not all bad either or the wards would have kicked him out.'

'The wards help kick out people who mean harm. They can still stay and be assholes,' Duncan said dryly.

'Well…yes,' Marge admitted. 'Can we follow them for a bit? I want to make sure if it is Marshall that he's okay. This is weird behavior for him.'

Duncan nodded and when the man and the tortoise got far enough away, he slowly followed them. It looked like Steve lived close to town, opposite end of the mechanic's shop though, closer to the park and Rolf's side of town. He was surprised that they hadn't run into him before. As soon as they reached Steve's backyard, Duncan slowed down to land in the neighbor's larger backyard. He and Marge watched as Steve ran the hose, letting the hot water flow out before filling a short bowl. It looked like an old dog bowl from here.

"There's plenty of grass and dandelions to eat," Steve said. "Eat all you want. I know it's a mess back here, but I can't bend for long to do the weeding."

'I suspected he still had pain sometimes from the accident, but I didn't know it was that bad,' Marge said.

'What type of accident was it?' Duncan asked.

'Something at work. I think large equipment or a truck or something was involved? The only thing people knew for sure was that it was at work. He never talked about it, and as you know, he isn't the friendliest. He was that way before the accident, but he became even more reclusive afterward,' Marge replied.

'What the hell is he doing now?' Duncan exclaimed.

Marge turned back to look and caught a glimpse of a tanned naked backside. 'I have no idea why he's shifting. Steve looks extremely alarmed.'

'I think I would be too if I suddenly had someone naked in front of me. Especially if I'd never seen anyone shift before,' Duncan replied. As much as he thought Steve was a dick, he could understand him being startled.

"What the fuck! Who are you?" Steve shouted, a little panicked.

'Should we intervene?' Duncan asked.

Marge shook her head. 'Let's wait. Marshall had to have had a reason.' Even if she had no idea what it could be.

"My name's Marshall. I own the mechanic shop at the end of town. Thank you for helping me."

"Uh. You're welcome? Why don't you have any clothes on?" Steve looked like he was trying his best to avoid looking anywhere south of Marshall's chin.

"I'm not one of the ones that can shift with clothes on. Not very many can." Marshall took a step closer, breathing deep. "Why haven't I seen you before? Are you new in town?"

"Uh, no. I've lived here a few years. I stick to my home and the library mostly. I work from home now and get my groceries delivered. And I take my car to the dealer," Steve said, still sounding nervous. His eyes still tried to slide down to look at the slim, tanned skin, dark-haired man in front of him. "What kind of turtle are you?"

"Bolson tortoise. There's not a lot of us. Regular ones are listed as endangered and have a small range now. We normally like deserts. Do you know about paranormals?"

"It's a bit late to ask that, don't ya think?" Steve asked sarcastically.

Marshall just waited.

"I found out a little bit ago. At the town meeting," Steve replied.

"Ah. I was out of town. Gage told me about it beforehand though. I'm sorry I missed you," Marshall said.

"I'm not. I was a bit of an ass," Steve admitted. "You really can't stand out here naked, man. You got any clothes?"

"Not here and I don't want to leave yet. I was in my backyard when I suddenly caught this most delightful scent and had to follow it," Marshall said, taking another step closer.

'Crap. How do you think this is going to go?' Duncan asked. Wanting to follow a scent that badly could only mean one thing.

Marge shrugged. She had no idea. This was not where she thought it would go though. What was with this town and people finding their mates?

"Have you heard of mates yet?" Marshall asked softly.

Steve shook his head, his eyes wide. Marge could smell his unease and burgeoning panic from here.

"Can we talk inside? I promise I will never hurt you. I know you don't have any reason to believe me but remember the wards. I think you're extremely special and I want to get to know you," Marshall said.

Steve scoffed. "I'm not special. But we can talk, I guess.

It's been a long time since I had a guest. I think I have some shorts that might fit you. I'm a bit bigger, so my shirts are going to be loose, but the shorts have a drawstring at least.

"That's fine, ma—man," Marshall followed him inside.

'I did not expect that,' Duncan admitted. *'Do you think he'll be alright, or should we stick around to make sure Marshall is safe?'*

'Steve isn't violent. Plus, Marshall is a shifter, so he'll be stronger than Steve. If there's even a slim, miniscule chance that Steve might accept his claim, I don't want to be here to hear it," Marge said.

Duncan nodded, curling his hand tighter around his mate before flapping his wings to gain elevation. He flew to the farthest outskirts of town before heading back home. Landing in the backyard, he noticed that most of the family was hanging out on the back patio. Ian and Berkley were at the grill, Doc and Emma were curled up on the couch, he saw some of the hammocks were full. There were now two pavilions with a total of eight hammocks and hammock chairs, enough for most of them. Rolf had told him that Shaye, Tess, and Emma usually preferred the chairs or the sofa. Rolf came out of the house holding a bag of ice, adding it to the cooler that sat off to the side. Shaye followed bringing out a plate of burgers, Tess with the condiments and a bag of buns.

"Where's Merri?" Marge asked. "I've got some tea."

"Really?" Tess asked, intrigued. "You guys just went flying. What kind of stuff could you have found out?"

Merri came out a minute later, carrying a book.

"Marge heard some gossip while they were out," Tess said. "Get over here so she can tell us!"

Merri shook her head at her sister but sat down in an open chair.

"We went flying and it was amazing. There were so many cool things in the woods. We even saw a bear. Thanks to Berkley's amazing pendant, we flew in town too. So, first. Did anyone else hear what happened in town today?"

Everyone shook their heads. Most of them had been here, except for Sam who had been working at the brewery.

"I heard Paul was speeding through town and Gage gave him a speeding ticket, but that's it," Sam said.

"Must have been after we saw him," Duncan said.

"He was speeding, and probably on his phone," Marge replied. "He almost ran over an animal, but Steve jumped in front of it and saved it from being run over."

"Huh. Wouldn't have picked him as an animal lover," Sam said. The man always seemed annoyed by everything.

"Did you know our local mechanic is a turtle?" Duncan asked.

"Tortoise actually," Marge corrected.

"No! Marshall was in the road? Why? He's never been that reckless," Doc said. He had known the tortoise shifter for quite a few years, both as a patient and as his mechanic.

"He apparently was tracking down a scent," Marge said with a smirk.

"Seriously? No way!" Sam leaned so far over the edge of his hammock he almost fell out. "He can't be…"

Marge nodded. "Steve brought the 'tortoise' home to let him eat the grass and get some water and Marshall shifted right there in his backyard. Fully naked, just standing there talking to Steve. When we left, they had just gone inside to talk," Marge said.

"I didn't even know Steve was gay. I don't think I've ever seen him date," Sam said. Whenever Steve had come into the brewery, he ate alone or got a single meal to go. He didn't even sit with a friend group.

"Doc, has he been in to see you lately?" Marge asked.

Doc shook his head. "I can't say much because of privacy laws, but I think the last time was right after his accident. I was fighting with the insurance to get them to cover his medical costs. I didn't charge for my time since they were being jerks about covering anything to do with it, especially the hospital bills. Why?"

"He made a comment when Marshall was still shifted that he should eat anything he wanted because he had a hard time bending to do any weeding. I had suspected that he might still have pain from some of the things I saw when he was in the library."

"I tried to schedule appointments with him, but he would cancel. He later told me he found a doctor near his car dealership and just went there when he took his car in."

Rolf got on his phone, typing a message out to someone.

"Gary's going to stop by and see if he can help with the yard. He does videos on how he manages weeds and yards. A lot of times he does the work for free in exchange for being able to use the yard as part of his promotions. He may be able to get Steve to accept his help at least this one time until we figure something out," Rolf said.

"Can Marshall change him, or is he one of the shifters that can't change someone?" Shaye asked.

No one answered for a minute.

"I'm not entirely sure," Marge admitted. "I don't know that I've dealt with many tortoise shifters."

Everyone else shook their heads.

"Well, if he can't change or chooses to stay human, maybe Marshall can talk him into seeing Doc again. I could help if he came into the office," Shaye said. They were keeping her healing abilities very quiet, but she hated to know he was suffering when she could help.

13

Marge was nervous. It was her first day back at work. She had been staying in Duncan's room at Rolf's house. She missed her apartment at the library, but at the same time she had really enjoyed staying here. As the Guardian, she felt obligated to live there to help protect it. Not that she had done such a great job when she had been attacked. She was still capable of looking after it, she told herself. She had held her ground and not taken the book out, and she had set up the wards in the first place.

Merri had told her that she was going to work with her today, even though Marge knew it was her day off. They were planning on going in early so that Marge would have time to reacclimate herself. Merri had promised the new computer screen had come in and everything had been cleaned up. It was a little disconcerting to realize that the 'everything' included your own blood.

"You can take one more day," Duncan told her.

She shook her head. "I really do need to reopen. It's summer reading time and the kids get so excited for the reading program. They earn different prizes based on how many books they read. Everyone who participates gets a free ice cream cone with their first turn-in."

"That sounds fun. Is there an adult one?" he asked curiously.

"No," she said slowly. "That's a good idea though. It might draw more people in and give them the chance to meet new people." She was thinking there were probably others besides Steve who were lonely and needed friends. "Maybe some large chocolate bars or movie tickets for prizes? I'll brainstorm today and come up with a plan. I can keep the adult version all year round too, since there's no tradition attached to it."

"Do you mind if I come with you today and check out the library?" he asked, trying to be casual about it. He could feel through their bond how nervous she was, and he wanted to be there if she needed him. He did want to see the library in its full glory and replace the image in his head of Marge's blood mixed with a broken lamp and a smashed computer screen.

"I know what you're doing," she said, looking at him. "But yes, come check it out. I can show you the back room since Merri can sit at the front desk. After we close, I'll show you my apartment."

Duncan was excited to see his mate's space. Although they both loved it at the Clan house, he thought she was drawn back to the library. Rolf had told him privately that no matter where they chose to live, they were always welcome at the house, and they would keep a room ready for them in case they ever wanted to stay the night. Plus, if they ever had a date night, Jimmy could stay at the house and be safe. They'd probably get him back hyped up on sugar and video games, depending on who would be watching him, but that was what family was for.

As they started to leave the house, he had her wait by the front door. Grabbing the present, he handed it to her, eager to see what she thought. She had loved flying, so hopefully she would love this too.

Marge looked at the box and then back at her mate. Opening it, she smiled as she realized it was a helmet. "Really? Are we taking it in today?"

Duncan nodded. "I have it ready to go out front. Sam drove Merri in on his way to the brewery and was going to stay with her until we got there. Gage checked it out and made sure everything was good last night. The wards are doing their job."

"Let's go," Marge said as she ran out the door.

It only took minutes to reach the library, but it was a fun experience. She couldn't wait until they could take the motorcycle out on a highway to really feel the rush of air going by her. Marge imagined it would feel a bit like flying had. She made a note to herself that they would need a shelter of some kind for his bike in the winter, unless they kept it stored at Rolf's. She knew that the big garage had been finished and now housed Gawain's Airstream and Ian's utility trailer from when he worked at Renaissance festivals. She would imagine there would be room for Duncan's bike. The lights were on, welcoming her back. Marge waved as they pulled around to park at the back, seeing Merri standing at the back door. Duncan noticed Sam standing just off to the side of the doorway. As Duncan walked inside, he realized that he hadn't been in this room yet. It was a break room from the looks of it; there were coffees, tea, and pastries from the bakery in town.

"Mary sent your favorite," Merri said, handing Marge a caramel macchiato and a warm almond filled croissant. "She wanted me to tell you if you need anything, even a snack, to let her know. She didn't want to crowd you, since she figured enough people were going to be doing that today, but wanted to let you know she's here to help in any way and she's glad you're home safe."

"That was nice of her," Marge replied, feeling touched.

"Duncan, they sent some things for you to pick from. Mary wasn't sure what your favorite was, but thought you'd be in here keeping Marge company. Here's your coffee," Merri said, handing him a cup.

"You guys need anything, call. Most of us are in town today, except for Rolf and Tess. They're both working from home. And of course, Emma's at home with Jimmy working on school stuff," Sam said as he headed out the door. "If you guys need a break, let us know. We can stand at the desk and point in the general direction of most things here."

"Thank you, Sam," Marge said, giving him a quick hug before he left.

She pulled out a seat, determined to enjoy her breakfast before facing the memories in the main room. She looked over as she felt a nudge on her shoulder. "I'm glad you're back," Merri said simply. The warm almond filling and the crustiness of croissant made Marge hum in happiness. The coffee was just a wonderful extra bonus. All too soon her food was gone, and she knew she had to face the other room. As she put her hand on the doorknob, Merri reached out to stop her.

"Hold on. I think you need these," she said with a grin before placing Marge's keys in her hand. "Welcome back, Guardian."

Marge had to blink back tears, because her sweet friend was letting her know that she believed in her, that she was telling Marge "you got this." She gave Merri a quick hug and turned quickly to yank open the door. This was her home, and she wasn't going to let some hunters scare her off, she told herself.

Walking into the room, her breath caught in her throat. Merri had already turned all the lights on so Marge wasn't walking into a darkened room. Looking around, she couldn't see any traces from the kidnapping. Duncan held her hand as she walked first to the paranormal section of the library, pressing her hand on the door. The wards flexed, warming beneath her hand, sending her vibes of welcome and joy. The library was happy she was home. Taking out her key, she opened the door, the three of them entering the room. Everything was just as she'd left it, and she felt a tension leave her body that she hadn't even realized she was carrying.

"We really need to go through these sooner rather than later. See what they wanted so desperately. It was a ledger of sorts and I remember seeing something that might fit that description when I did a quick look through the box. If we can figure out exactly what it is, maybe it will give us an edge to dealing with them," Marge said. She led the way back out, locking the door behind her. She was thinking maybe it was time to give Merri her own key. If anything happened to Marge, then all that knowledge would be lost until another Guardian was appointed. She took a deep breath and slowly walked to the help desk. It looked in perfect condition, no sign of the struggle or fighting that had occurred. All the mess had been cleaned up, the computer screen brand new and ready to use, the lamp replaced. She liked the new lamp; it had a colorful glass mosaic shade that cast little rainbows around the area. It was cheerful and bright.

Marge stood behind the desk, looking around. She could do this. This was her space. "Let's get the doors open for the day. I'm sure the kids are anxious to catch up on the summer reading program. Duncan, if we get really busy, I may need you to help with prizes. When they turn their sheet in, they get to pick a prize from different levels based on how much they read. All the boxes are labeled. If it's their first turn-in, then they also get a token for a free ice cream cone. It would be marked off on their sheet if they already got one. Let me go grab the boxes and we can set you up at the table over here." Normally she had the boxes in the kids' area, but she knew Duncan would want to be able to keep an eye on her. And truthfully, she wanted that too. She ran him through the process quickly, finishing just in time for the clock to chime indicating it was time to open.

Merri went to open the doors, giving a look at Marge when she got a glimpse outside. She made a wait gesture and shut the door to yell back at Marge, "You need to see this."

Duncan stood halfway between the desk and the door, close enough to get to his mate quickly, but giving her enough space to do this on her own. When Merri threw both doors all the way open, he could see several people waiting on the steps, many with flowers or balloons, some with what looked like bags from the bakery, little kids holding stuffed animals or cards. He didn't know these people, but even he was getting a little choked up with emotion. His mate was clearly well liked, and he didn't think she had been aware of how much she meant to these people based on the surprised gasp and a few sniffles. She quickly wiped at her eyes and moved to the open doorway.

"Is it someone's birthday?" she asked, jokingly, trying to make light of her quick tears.

A little girl came running up, grabbing one of Marge's legs in a hug. "I'm glad you're back, Miss Marge. I missed you."

Marge crouched down, giving the girl a hug. "I missed you too. Did you get to the next level of your reading?"

"I did! I'm ready for a prize," the little girl said proudly.

"My…boyfriend is in there helping today. He looks big and scary, but he's really nice. He's in charge of prizes, if you want to turn your sheet in. You'll be the first one today!"

"Thank you!" she yelled as she ran into the building.

Merri touched her shoulder, leaning in to whisper. "I'll handle the desk. You greet your adoring fans. They've all been asking us about you." Marge nodded, squeezing her hand back.

It was a steady stream of well wishes. Some of the patrons didn't even go inside the library, they simply wanted to see her and give her something. She had no idea what she was going to do with so many stuffed animals, but she figured she could decorate the desk, leave some for others to enjoy in the children's area, and bring some home to Jimmy. She had a feeling he hadn't been given a lot of toys in his life. The boy was excited about the book of word finds that Doc had given him, for goodness' sake.

At lunchtime, Merri thrust a container in her hands and gave her a shove toward the break room.

"Go eat, get a break. It's been busy today. Gawain is coming over to help with the prize bins, so take Duncan with you. Enjoy some of the food everyone brought. If you're still hungry, Sam said to send him a text and he'll have someone run food over."

Marge gave her friend a quick hug. "Thanks," she said. Looking around, there was a lull in what had been a steady stream of visitors. She almost ran to the children's prize table to grab her mate, dragging him toward the break room.

Duncan laughed. "Where are we going?"

"Merri has Gawain coming over, so we can get a break," Marge said, stopping in the doorway to the break room. "Good lord. How are we going to eat this all?" Even with a shifter's appetite, there was no way she could eat all of this.

"We can bring a lot of it home. Jimmy would certainly like to try new foods. And the guys can eat a lot. We can put some of the cookies out at the desk with a sign. Something like 'thanks for welcoming me back, please help me eat all of these treats' or something. We can run some over to Gage too, or if he stops by, have him pick some out to take home," Duncan said.

"That's a good idea," Marge replied. She grabbed a couple muffins and pulled him into her office.

Duncan looked around. It was cozy in here, bookcases and filing cabinets took up one wall. She had a large old wood desk, but the chair was a newer model, more ergonomic. She had different book-themed posters around the room. There was a cork board filled with Post-its and other reminders. Little statues of dragons and cats were scattered about the room. He touched one, looking at her, raising an eyebrow.

Marge laughed softly. "I've always had a thing for dragons," she admitted.

Duncan grabbed her by the waist, pulling her closer. "Good to know," he smirked, leaning his head down to give her a kiss. He meant to keep it short, just a brief kiss, but it quickly escalated. They hadn't had a lot of time to be intimate yet, with her recovering and then Jimmy having nightmares would often come into their room at night.

He felt her nails sharpen, turning to her cat's claws, grabbing at him but not cutting into his skin. Her tongue rasped against his, her breasts pushed firmly into his chest, the nipples already a little hard. His cock filled, leaving him wanting more. He wanted to be deep in his mate, feel her warmth surrounding him, letting him know they were together, and she was safe and alive with him. He had almost lost her before he found her, and he didn't think that feeling of desperation would leave him anytime soon.

Marge broke off the kiss, staring into his eyes. *'I'm fine, love,'* she told him. *'Let's go. I'm not having sex in my office, there's too many piles to knock over.'*

'I thought kitties loved to knock things over,' he teased. He quietly sighed and reached down to adjust his length. He needed to plan a night where someone could watch Jimmy and they could have some together time, he thought to himself as he started walking toward the door.

"Where are you going?" Marge asked.

"Back to the break room," he said, a slight question in his voice.

Marge shook her head, a smile on her face.

"You said no office sex, and I get it. Come on, I'll feed you," Duncan said.

Marge stepped up to her silly man, giving him a kiss with

a quick grope. "I didn't say no sex, just no office sex. Wait." Reaching out, she pushed a couple books around and a secret door opened up, revealing a staircase leading to the basement. "Let's go to my apartment," she said, flipping on the light switch.

Duncan was stunned. He had no idea that was even there. How cool was that? He pulled the door shut behind them, following her down the stairs. It looked like a normal basement, but his dragon told him there were caves nearby. He'd have to explore the area, see if there were any places big enough for his dragon to hang out. Reaching the bottom of the stairs, there was another door. Marge opened it, no lock in sight. He might have to look at the security of the doors, especially after her attack.

'There are wards on both doors. Don't worry. No one could get down here if I didn't want them to,' Marge said.

Duncan walked through the doorway, hit with the scent of his mate. There was a faint scent of Merri, but it seemed like no one else had been down here. His inner caveman was pleased. There was a comfy-looking couch with a few soft knitted blankets thrown over the back, a recliner, a kitchen with a small table, lots of bookshelves, and two doors. Probably the bathroom and bedroom, if he had to guess.

"It's not huge, but it's home. If Jimmy stays with us, we'll have to figure out how to build another bedroom and bathroom down here. Or I'll have to move my library room. It used to be a second bedroom attached to the Master," Marge said, worrying her bottom lip with her teeth.

"We'll figure it out. I'm sensing caves, so maybe we could expand into one of those, put in a good support structure and wards to keep it safe. I'm pretty handy when it comes to building things."

14

"That's a good idea," Marge said. She took a look at her mate, standing in her home. The whole library was her space, but this area was just hers. Well, theirs. She had never felt that her home was too small, although it fell into the tiny home type of square footage, but with Duncan in here, it felt smaller. She took a moment to admire his six-foot four-inch frame, his dark hair, those gorgeous gray eyes, and the markings on his body. He was in an emerald t-shirt today, the tight sleeves making his biceps pop. He was wearing a pair of dark bootcut jeans, the jeans cupping his butt, his muscular thighs barely contained in the fabric, his feet encased in black biker boots. The boots, beard, and markings made him look like the quintessential bad boy, but she knew what a softy he was. Not that he couldn't hold his own in a fight, because well, dragon.

Reaching out, she softly trailed a finger down his nose, his lips, his chest. His breathing picked up a little as she gently pinched a nipple. Using her whole hand, she rubbed down his chest, down his six pack, teasing along the waistband of his pants. Duncan adjusted, spreading his legs a bit wider. Marge barely glanced over the bulge forming in the front of his pants before walking around to his backside. She smiled at his groan, but she was going to enjoy having her mate to herself right now. Sliding her hands under his shirt, she slowly worked the material up. Duncan lifted his arms, pulling it the rest of the way off.

Marge ran her hands over his skin, loving how smooth it was, her fingers tracing the dips and grooves of his muscles. She looked for the hidden wing marking, leaning in to press her lips to it. Kissing down his back, she slid her hands around his waist, unbuckling his belt to slide his pants down his thighs. Duncan tilted his hips, chasing after her touch. She reached into his boxers, gently rubbing her fingertips across his hard length, teasing around the head. Marge held his shaft in her hand as she walked around in front of him, pressing her lips to his as she slowly stroked his cock. She didn't apply too much pressure, just enough to keep him hard but not coming. Duncan's hand found its way under her shirt, unsnapping her bra to gain access to her breasts. He played with her nipples, rubbing his thumb over one and then the other, taking turns. His tongue was playing with hers, twisting together, with the occasional nip to her lips. Marge pulled back to get a deep breath before dropping to her knees in front of him. There was no way she could fit all of him in her mouth, she still had a gag reflex, but she was going to give it her best shot. Looking up at him, she slowly ran her tongue the length of his shaft, teasing the slit at the top. She leaned away to rip her shirt and bra off, her nipples hardening instantly in the cooler air.

Unzipping her pants, she slid them to sit below her butt, knowing her lacy thong would be highlighting her cheeks. Leaning forward, she slowly drew his dick into her mouth, her hands resting on his muscular thighs. Tracing the patterns there, she took him in as deep as she could, bumping the back of her throat. She was learning what he liked best, and she drew back to settle into a good rhythm with her head bobs, moving her tongue back and forth across his shaft. His hands moved to clench in her hair, tightening, but not pulling or forcing her to take him deeper. She moved her left hand to cup his balls, her thumb slowly stroking back and forth across the wiry hairs and sensitive skin. Duncan moaned, his hips thrusting a little. She lightly ran her fingertips over his sac, causing it to tighten. She knew he was getting close. Her right hand gripped the base of his shaft, slowly moving up and down. Between her mouth and her hand, she had him almost completely covered.

"No, babe. I want to be in you when I come," Duncan grunted, pulling away from her mouth.

"You were in me," she stated, quirking an eyebrow at him.

Duncan leaned down, picking her up to throw her over his shoulder before walking to the bedroom. Which was pretty funny from her angle since he still had his pants around his ankles.

"Oh!" she gasped when she felt a light tap to her ass.

"No laughing at me," he grumbled.

"Well, your pants are around your ankles," she pointed out, lightly smacking his cheeks as they flexed in front of her.

Duncan tossed her on the bed, pouncing on her as soon as she landed, ripping her pants and shoes off before getting rid of his own. She saw the monster of his dick, precum dripping from the tip, and she wanted another taste.

"Uh uh," he said, shaking his head. "It's my turn."

Kneeling on the floor, he gently spread her legs, running his nose up one leg, breathing in deep as he reached her mons. "You always smell so good, mate." He lightly ran a finger over her slit, not quite firm enough to slide between her folds. His tongue barely touched her, teasing her with the sensation. He reached up, cupping both of her breasts, his thumbs leisurely stroking. As his tongue breached her crease, she squirmed, trying to get closer, to get his tongue where she wanted it. Whimpering, she wrapped her legs around him, pulling him in. His tongue licked, circling her clit before dipping down to her entrance. She could feel the wetness growing as he worked her body. All of a sudden, his tongue speared into her, longer and more flexible than she thought it should be. She screamed as it found her G-spot, rubbing against it. His tongue felt textured, a little rougher, and it felt amazing against her sensitive passage. Her body was screaming for release, she was so close. She sobbed as it suddenly felt heated, much warmer than it had been a moment ago, twisting to thrust into her depths while the tip pressed on her G-spot. She screamed as his thumb came down to press against her clit, her climax punching through her, making her see black spots with the intensity of her orgasm. She lay there, gasping for breath, his tongue still gently stroking her, causing mini orgasms. Marge pulled his hair to get him to come up for air.

"Wh—" she cleared her throat. "What was that?" she asked.

"You're not the only one who can partially shift," he said smugly.

"Yay for me," she cheered, still feeling tingles.

Duncan pressed upwards, leaning over her. "Love you," he said simply before kissing her tenderly.

It only took a couple of minutes of kissing and caressing before she was eager to have him finish what they started. She could feel his hard length pressing into her skin, dripping and leaving little marks of precum over her legs. She would have to wipe down before she went back upstairs. The bad thing about having so many other paranormals around was their great sense of smell.

Marge lifted her legs to wrap around his waist, pulling him into her while she lifted her hips. Duncan reached down, pulling her closer, getting the perfect angle for him to slide into her body.

He groaned as she clenched her muscles tight around him, holding him within her.

"You feel so good," he said, holding himself still, wanting to make this last.

Marge wrapped her hands behind his neck, pulling him down for a kiss. Her tongue thrust into his mouth, claiming him for her own, her teeth nipping at him gently, urging him to move. He started slowly, his hips gliding back and forth, keeping his lips near hers, their breaths mingling. Marge dug her heels into his back, "Faster. Duncan. Please," she pleaded, so close to coming again. His dick filled her completely, hitting her G-spot perfectly as he thrust harder into her welcoming body. This. This was perfect, she thought, her hands grabbing at his back, her nails scratching his skin. Her body was so close to flying.

Duncan moved his head, biting into her mating mark and Marge screamed as pleasure rushed through her whole body. "Yes! Love you," she gasped out as she felt his cock swell inside her, filling her with his heat.

He collapsed over top of her, careful to keep most of his weight supported on his elbows. "That was amazing," he said finally, pressing a kiss to her forehead.

"It was," she agreed, pressing a kiss to his chest. "I think we need a shower though."

Duncan laughed but stood up, scooping her up in his arms before walking to the bathroom.

15

Marge walked into the Clan house, wondering where everyone was. She was late today. Duncan had been at the apartment planning out the expansion, but he had left early to get measurements for things he wanted to move in. They wouldn't move Jimmy in until they had the all clear from Gage, so it gave them time to get everything ready. If they did find his parents and they were decent people, Duncan could always use it as an office and having another bathroom was never a bad thing. She wondered where he was; Duncan should have beaten her home.

She frowned, a little disappointed that she was here alone. They had talked last week about her joining the Clan tonight. Maybe they had forgotten, she thought, her heart aching. For someone who had been alone for so long, she had quickly come to look forward to the family gatherings.

Shaking her head, she dropped her things on the couch before heading toward the kitchen. She would just throw a pizza in the oven and Duncan could share when he came home.

"Surprise!" A myriad of voices rang out when she flipped

on the light switch. A small body came barreling toward her, almost knocking her to the ground.

"Oof," she grunted, wrapping her arms around Jimmy.

"Isn't this so cool?" he asked excitedly. "I've never been to a surprise party before!"

"Me either," she admitted quietly. Marge looked around, seeing all of her adopted family gathered in the kitchen, including her smiling mate. Sam and Ian had on crazy party hats and were blowing noise makers. There were cupcakes and other foods along the counter, a pitcher of what looked like strawberry margaritas, and a crudité platter.

"It's not my birthday," she said slowly, trying to figure out what was going on.

"Nope, but it's your joining-the-Clan day," Shaye said with a smile, handing her a drink.

"You cannae get rid of us now," Ian teased.

"Oh! Thank you," Marge said, feeling her cheeks heat up. No one had ever thrown her a party.

Rolf walked over. "We can wait, if you're not ready," he said, thinking her pause was hesitation.

"No, I'm ready. I can't wait to be part of this family," Marge replied quickly.

"You're already part of the family, regardless if you join the Clan," Rolf replied with a smile. "You pick. Do you want to do it before or after we eat? I'm good either way."

"Before," she replied. She knew what she wanted, so there was no reason to delay it any longer.

Marge felt a stirring along her mind, and she let down her guards enough for Rolf to initiate the telepathic link.

'I pledge fealty to my Clan leader, Rolfston of the Nightwood Clan,' Marge vowed.

Rolf gently bit her, choosing to bite on the opposite side of her neck, as far away from her mating mark as possible. *'I accept you into my Clan,'* he replied.

Marge staggered for a second, feeling everyone at once.

"It takes a bit to get used to," Ian told her. "Just ah, be careful which link you're talking on," he advised, his face red.

Tess snorted and Sam just lost it, laughing hysterically.

"What'd I miss?"

"Back when we first had the Clan link, none of us were used to it. Some of us," Shaye said, stressing the word while looking at Ian, "may have accidentally used the wrong link during, um, special times," she finished, her own face turning pink.

Special ti—Oh! Sex. Marge pressed her lips together, trying to keep her laughter in but lost the fight as Duncan started laughing.

"Yeah, fun times," Berkley said dryly, his own cheeks pinkened.

Emma shook her head at them. "Alright, let's leave poor Ian alone. Food's ready," she said, trying to herd them into getting their plates.

Marge loaded up, touched that they had made a lot of her favorite foods. She helped clean up after everyone was done eating, looking forward to relaxing. The library hadn't been open long today, since it was Sunday, but in the past, she had always taken Sundays by herself, knowing Merri had the Clan's family dinner. She might have to bump up closing by an hour to make sure she would make it on time from now on, she thought. She didn't want to miss dinner and game night.

Ian had been wonderful and bought a bunch of kid-friendly games so Jimmy could play too. They had played *Ticket To Ride Junior* last week, Doc playing on Jimmy's team. It was adorable seeing Doc whisper pointers and tips to help him win. It was getting harder to find games that could accommodate all of them, so they had started pairing up depending on the game. Marge thought maybe it would be *Sorry* or *Monopoly* tonight, based on his interest in them last week.

"What do ye feel like playing tonight?" Ian asked, standing by the game cabinet, ready to pull anything out.

Jimmy walked over to look at his options. "What do you do with these?" he asked, holding up a simple deck of cards.

"So many things!" Ian said excitedly.

"Like what?" Jimmy asked, opening the box and staring at the contents suspiciously. "They just look like shiny paper."

"They do," Ian agreed. "But there's lots of card games we can teach you. Crazy Eights, Go Fish, Euchre, Rummy, Solitaire, BS, Hearts. Some poker when you're older," he added with a wink, ignoring Marge's raised eyebrow.

"Can we play Go Fish?" he asked after thinking about it for a minute.

"Sure," Ian replied. "Card games can be lots of fun. I'll show you how to build a house with them after we're done playing."

Emma was the last one to find a seat, placing a few bowls of snacks around the living room. They may need to get a bigger coffee table, if they were going to keep playing in here, Marge thought. It was a bit crowded with all of them gathered around, especially when Rockefeller came in looking for any snacks that might have fallen to the floor. The wolfdog was not lap sized any more, although he certainly seemed to think he was.

They managed to teach Jimmy Go Fish, Crazy Eights, and Hearts before he started nodding off at the table.

"I'll go put him in bed," Marge said, bending over to pick him up.

"Do you guys want to have an Inebriated Inconsistencies night? I'm not quite ready for bed and I saw a commercial for an absolutely ridiculous documentary," Gawain said, disgust in his tone.

Marge looked at Duncan and nodded. She was eager to see what the game was like. She had heard a few stories from Merri, and it sounded very entertaining.

"We're in," Duncan said. "I'll help get drinks ready," he offered, giving Marge a kiss before helping clean up the cards and the empty snack bowls.

Marge climbed up the stairs, trying not to wake the boy. Shifting his weight to one arm, she managed to get the door open, and the covers pulled down. Laying him gently on the bed, she tucked his feet under the covers before pulling them up.

"I don't think my parents love me," Jimmy said quietly.

Marge was taken aback and sat back to look at his face. She had thought he was still asleep. "Why do you say that?"

"They didn't act like everyone here does. They didn't touch each other much, we never had TV night or game night. Most of the time, I didn't even eat dinner with them. They said it was because they ate really late and I had school, but what if it was because they didn't like me?" he asked in a tiny voice.

"I think you're very likeable," Marge said. "Definitely loveable. Gage is still trying to find them and if he finds out that they won't be good parents, we can talk about our options then. Okay? All of us here want what's best for you and we're going to make sure you get it."

"Can I join the Clan?"

"Um," Marge said, pausing, not expecting that question. "I know they would all love to have you, but I think we have to wait on news on your parents first, kiddo. If they're great people, they're going to want you back. If they're not, then Gage will find a way you can stay with us, and we'll ask Rolf then. I know he would say yes," she tried to reassure him. "Either way, we'll always be your friends and there to help you."

"Okay," he said, his eyes closing again as sleep took him.

Marge sat there for a moment, ensuring he was asleep before kissing his head and making sure the nightlight was on, before easing the door shut and heading downstairs. She could hear laughter and the sounds of the TV. As she came into the room, she saw Gawain looking for the show, a row of drinks all lined up with a few more snacks. Everyone had moved from sitting on the floor around the coffee table to the couches and chairs. Well, except for Ian who was sitting on the floor between Berkley's legs, and Tess was sitting on Sam's lap.

She cuddled next to Duncan, tucking her feet underneath her. Gawain hit pause as there was a knock on the front door.

'They called and invited Gage,' Duncan told her.

'Oh, that's nice. I'm sure he'll love this,' Marge replied. Her oldest friend was just as much in need of a loving group of friends as she had been. She knew he had held himself back in the past because of his Warden status, but she didn't think that would make much difference to the people here. They liked him for who he was, not his position.

Gage walked in, carrying a few grocery bags. "I stopped and grabbed some snacks," he said. "How has everyone been doing?"

"Good," Rolf said, looking around the room, checking in on everyone.

Marge nodded. "Jimmy's been settling in well. I think he's anxious to go to school or come to the library, but I told him it needs to wait until we find out about his parents."

Emma spoke up. "I think if I keep working with him, we can have him evaluated before the next school year starts and see where he's at. He's learning extremely quickly. If he still needs to catch up, I'm happy to keep working with him and we can find some activities that would have other kids for him to meet. I know there's a soccer team that is non-competitive, and I think there may be a baseball team too. If he hasn't shifted yet, he can probably pass for human enough to play. We'd just have to make sure he doesn't accidently use his TruthSpeak on anyone."

Gage nodded. "I'll keep working with him on how to

shield his gift. He's been doing really well. Marco thinks he found a lead. One of the neighbors reached out and said they remembered being in their backyard and overhearing the parents talking about moving. He thought they mentioned something about hating cold weather but at least they'd get some good lobster to eat. We're thinking Maine, since it's both cold and has lobster."

"Maybe the northern part of California, or that part of Canada between Washington and Alaska? Are there lobsters there?" Sam asked.

"Could be, I'll have to look into it. I know California has spiny lobsters, but I'm not sure how far up they go. Marco had a faint scent and he's going to use that to try to trace them when he gets to Maine."

"It's a good place to hide," Berkley said. "There's a lot of wildernesses. I think over eighty percent of the state is wooded. It'd be easy to hide from people. Do you think they're by themselves or hiding with a group?"

"At this point, I have no idea. I know Barry is involved, but he's been amazing at covering his tracks. He's not dumb. Which makes it harder for us. We're also trying to keep it quiet; we don't need to be spooking him even more. Right now, he may think that it was the town that came together to look for Marge, or maybe that it was just her mate that got lucky enough to find her. If the Convocation got wind of what we were doing, there would be at least a couple of other members who would get in our way. We know Barry has two cronies there, based on what Rob and Gawain told us. He may have more that would back him simply because they don't want us looking into Convocation members' business. I know we would have support as well, but I figured it's better to not stir the pot quite yet. It means we're going slower than we should, but if this corruption is widespread, I want to be able to weed it all out and know the players before acting."

"That makes sense." Rolf nodded. "It won't do much good

long-term if we only get Barry out if there are others like him."

Marge bit her lip, wondering if she should bring up keeping the boy now, or wait until they had news on his parents. She knew Duncan had already approached Gage on it, but she liked having all the information available so she knew what the correct path would be.

"I know Duncan mentioned it to you, but if his parents are dead or working with Barry and it's not safe for him to go back, we would like to adopt him. What would we need to do for that?" she asked.

"I've already started looking into past cases where a paranormal was adopted. If his parents are still alive, we may have to fudge a few things to make it work. This is his home. Marco and I both believe that. He'd have a great family here, lots of support from a paranormal standpoint, and could go to school. Since the town knows about us now, it would be safe for him to keep going to school even after he shifts. He's already been to a human school, so that won't be a big adjustment either.

"I left a message for Rob to give me a call. I want to see just how high up his Convocation contact is. If they turn out to be a Convocation member, or even one of their assistants, we may be able to use them to adjust the records and slip the adoption into the system without drawing any attention to it. Don't worry. If his parents turn out to be rotten or passed away, we'll make sure he can stay here," Gage reassured her.

"Thank you," Marge said, feeling a little bit of relief. She hadn't even realized how much she had been worrying about it until he spoke.

"You're one of us. We'll help any way we can too," Shaye said, squeezing her shoulder. Marge felt the calming vibes Shaye was sending her and gave her a smile.

"Thanks," she said. "Now, give me one of those cookies,"

she demanded of Gage, trying to break the tension and bring back the relaxed atmosphere from before.

Gawain waited until Gage found his seat before passing out the drinks. "Everyone remember the rules? Find something wrong in the documentary, share with the group, and take a drink."

Fifteen minutes into the show, Marge was beyond grateful that they all had faster metabolisms. Merri and Tess were taking smaller sips since they were closer to human physiology. This was the worst piece of garbage she had seen in a long time. Did the producers research anything?

She laughed as all the guys shouted "No!" at the TV at the same time.

"Come on! That one was obvious! You could have looked it up in a book!" Gawain shouted, throwing his popcorn at the screen, sending Rockefeller scrambling to gobble up the pieces. "I should send them a scathing letter," he said, his words slurring just a little bit as he fumbled to get his phone out of his pocket.

"Maybe tomorrow," Merri said, laughing at him, subtly taking his phone away from him.

Gage laughed, the sound loud and carefree. It was a good look on her oldest friend.

16

A throat cleared, causing Marge to look up, startled. She had been so distracted by the new book order she was placing that she hadn't even heard anyone come in. She had been trying to get some new young adult books ordered so she would have more options for when Jimmy came in to visit. Until then, she would check the books out and bring them home for him. Rolf didn't have a lot of kid books, although she had noticed more and more appearing in his library. She thought it was very sweet how they all had adopted Jimmy. He now had a workspace on the first floor of the library with his own desk and school supplies, including a white board.

"Sorry," he said, looking a little sheepish. "I thought you heard me."

"Steve? Sorry, I was ordering new books. What can I do for you?" Marge asked. She thought she spied the tail end of a mating mark right under his collar. He still smelled human though, so she didn't think he had changed yet.

"Um. I, uh, was looking for a book," he stumbled through his words.

"Well, you came to the right place." She tried to make a corny joke to put him at ease, but it only seemed to fluster him more. His cheeks went red, and he looked down at the desk instead of at her.

"I'm, ah. I'm glad you're back," he said, shifting on his feet, fidgeting a bit. He was clearly still nervous about something.

"Thank you," Marge replied softly. She wished she knew how to make him feel better. "What kind of book are you looking for?"

"You're…um. You're a shifter, right?" he asked in a whisper, leaning in to make sure no one could overhear.

Marge nodded, a little amused since she knew the whole town was aware of her shifter status after the townhall meeting when she was missing.

"I wanted…I was looking for…" Steve kept trailing off.

"He wanted to say he was sorry for his outburst at the townhall meeting. And to ask if you had any books on human mates to shifters and what changing species meant," a deep gruff voice rumbled.

Marge saw Marshall, the tortoise shifter, standing behind Steve, a hand on his back. She had to admit they made a cute couple. Steve was shorter by several inches, although Marshall was tall and built like a brick house. He was broad-shouldered, had a full bushy black beard and closely cropped hair. He looked almost like a biker. He was always quiet, great at his job, stopped into the library sometimes. Marge thought it was funny that the two men had never run into each other before.

"I don't, but I know somewhere that does. Give me one minute to get Merri," she said. "And congratulations."

'Merri, is there anyone at the museum today?' Marge reached out over the Clan link, before realizing she probably should have called to keep up appearances. *'Crap. Hold on, I'm going to call you.'* She heard Merri laughing.

Grabbing her phone, she called her friend. "Hey, I had a customer looking for a book that I think you have. Is there anyone there today?"

"I just checked. Shaye, Gawain, and Rolf are there. Shaye had the day off and was helping get some of the things put into the computer system for the gift shop," Merri replied. She was working in the back room of the library, sorting through the books that had been delivered weeks ago.

"Can I send someone down for help?" Marge asked.

"Who is it? We're not officially open yet, but there's probably enough stuff available to help."

'Steve and Marshall. They were looking for a book on human mates and what changing species meant.' Marge used the link so she wouldn't embarrass Steve any more.

'Oh. Wow. Yeah, send them down. Shaye would probably be good for him to meet anyway. She was human and a lot of this was her idea. She's been looking for an excuse to bump into him too. I think she's hoping she can help with his pain,' Merri said. *'Why don't I cover the front desk. I'll call Duncan to come upstairs if I need help. I think you're the one Steve would be the most comfortable with, so maybe you can walk them down?'*

"That's a good idea. I'll wait until you get here," Marge replied.

Turning back to Steve, who looked like he wanted to run, Marge told him, "They're going to let you in, even though they're not open yet. As soon as Merri gets here to cover the front desk, I can walk you down."

"Oh no. That's okay. We can come back another day," Steve said nervously.

"Nope. Not doing that again. You're going to get your answers so we can move on. You can't keep running away and hiding from me," Marshall said, exasperated.

"I'm here! I let them know you're on your way," Merri said, walking up to the desk.

Marge led them out of the building, noticing that Steve

was limping badly today. She slowed her pace so she wouldn't put more stress on his body. It didn't take them long to reach their destination and she knocked on the door.

"Paranormal History Museum? What is this? It's not a joke," Steve said angrily.

Marge was saved from answering when Rolf opened the door. "Come on in," he said, holding the door open for them.

Marshall gently herded his mate into the building, Rolf locking it behind them.

"Let's go upstairs," Rolf said. "Shaye and Gawain were getting a few things ready for you."

Shaye was waiting for them at the top of the stairs, anxiously looking at Steve. "Come sit down," she offered, grabbing his arm to guide him into the room. She sat next to him, holding one of his hands.

Steve looked startled by the whole thing, but Marge grinned. Marshall was bristling at the sight of someone touching his mate, especially someone he didn't really know.

"Just wait," Marge whispered to him. "She's safe."

It took a couple of minutes, Steve looking uncomfortable and like he wanted to pull his hand away. He looked back at Marshall for help, who simply made the stay-there gesture.

Marge watched as the tension lines around Steve's eyes and mouth smoothed out, his body relaxing and sitting better. Finally, Shaye's eyes opened, and she patted his hand before moving out of the seat so Marshall could sit next to his mate. Rolf ushered Shaye to the other side of the table, bringing her a candy bar and a water.

"What did you do?" Steve asked, amazement and a touch of fear in his voice.

"What? What happened?" Marshall asked, looking around for answers.

"She did something," Steve exclaimed. "I. I don't feel any pain. It's gone. I haven't felt this good in years, before the accident."

Shaye had her mouth full of Snickers and pointed at Rolf.

He shook his head at her but answered anyway. "Some paranormals," he began but cleared his throat when Shaye smacked his arm lightly. "And humans," he amended, "have special gifts or talents. Shaye can help heal. She's been waiting to run into you to help, but you never came into the clinic."

"She healed me? I'm all better?"

Shaye swallowed her last bite. "Almost. You have a little more nerve damage in your hip and leg, but I'll be able to fix that in a second. I hadn't eaten today and couldn't do it all in one go. Let me grab another snack and I'll finish."

"Thank you," Steve said quietly.

Shaye nodded, already eating a sandwich.

"That's not why you came in here though, is it?" Gawain asked.

"Uh. No. See, I didn't know anything about paranormals or shifters before the townhall. And it scared me a bit and I was an asshole. Then I save this tortoise from being hit by a car and suddenly there's this naked man standing in front of me telling me I'm his mate and stuff. I trust him, but I…"

"Wanted to know more before you made a big decision," Shaye guessed. "Yeah. I keep telling these guys they need a "So you mated a paranormal" book. That's the real purpose of the museum, to help other people. The downstairs has some truth to it, but the real stuff isn't kept down there. Did Marshall explain mating?"

Steve nodded. "You can stay human and not mate, mate and get an increased lifespan, or mate and change. But I don't know if I want to be a tortoise. It sounds like it would hurt."

Marshall shook his head behind him, clearly having had this conversation many times.

"Well, I think Marshall wanted you to change so you would get the extra healing abilities as a shifter. He was probably hoping it would help your pain." She held out a hand, which Steve slowly took. Shaye closed her eyes again, this time more briefly. "There. Now you're all healed. This will take care of your pain problem, but if you are only mated, you will not get any of the extra abilities that shifters have. I was human last year and chose to turn. I wanted to be able to protect my mate, and getting easily injured because I was essentially human wouldn't do that. As far as I know, shifting doesn't hurt," she looked over to Gawain.

"No, it doesn't hurt. You can feel it, but it's not painful," Gawain said.

Rolf pulled out some pamphlets to give to Steve. "This is some of the information we've been working on getting together. I don't have ones specific to tortoises, sorry. None of us know that much about them. Shaye's putting together a guidebook of sorts as we go along."

Now that he wasn't in constant pain, Steve seemed a lot more relaxed and started asking them questions. They answered the best they could. Marge thought it made him feel better having another human who had mated a paranormal to talk to. Marshall even filled out a tortoise page in Shaye's book.

When they left, Steve reached out and grabbed Marshall's hand, walking straight and evenly, no sign of the limp.

"That was amazing," Marge said. "I can't wait until this is open for real. I better get back to help Merri close down. I'll see you guys at dinner."

She made a quick stop at the bakery to grab some coffee and a tea for Merri, as well as a box of mixed cookies for dessert.

"Thank you for covering," Marge said, handing the tea over.

"How did it go?" Merri asked.

"Good. He had a lot of questions. He wanted to believe Marshall so badly, but needed some reassurance from others, I think."

"Did Shaye get a hold of him?"

"Yup. It was like a completely different man walking out. He seemed happier."

"I'd imagine not being in constant pain would make anyone happier. I'm glad they could help," Merri said, closing down the computer. "What kind of cookies did you get?"

"A little bit of everything. I told Jimmy I'd bring him one home if he studied really hard today. He's really hoping to go to school."

"He's been progressing so quickly, and I know that missing two years seems like a lot, but I think he's close enough to go. When is his evaluation?" Merri asked.

"Two weeks. He's nervous, but I think Duncan is even more so. He doesn't want Jimmy to be disappointed if they say to wait."

"Even if they do, we'll find some way to get him around other kids. There's bound to be some clubs or sports he can take part in," Merri said.

Marge nodded and locked up behind them, shifting the box of cookies to her other hand.

"How's the renovations coming in the apartment?" Merri asked. She was curious to see what it turned out like. She had seen it before and though it was a cute space, there definitely wasn't enough room for all three of them. At least not with an almost-teenaged boy. She remembered her brothers and they always were on the move.

"It's going really well. Duncan found a whole cave system that we can tap into. I want to get some wards on the area because I think his dragon is going to claim it as his space. There are several caverns that are large enough to hold him. He's explored it a bit and says it seems safe and there's all kinds of stalactites and stalagmites for Jimmy to find. Once we get it finished, I'll bring you down to see," Marge offered.

"I'd love that. We can get together with Gage and work on

wards for it. Does it lead outside at all, or is it all underground?" Merri asked.

"Right now, it looks like all underground. There's an area with a little pool and stream, but we haven't found an access point to aboveground yet. I think it's just a smaller area that formed over time."

"That's pretty cool," Merri said.

Marge thought about the cave. She should put in a door to the caverns, so it provided another barrier between them and the caves. Duncan had found it when digging out what was supposed to be Jimmy's new room to the right of her current bedroom. With the discovery of the caves, Marge was rethinking that plan. She didn't want him wandering into the caves without them and having access from his bedroom seemed like a bad idea. She could move the library and if they sealed off the connecting door to her bedroom and created a new door leading to the living room, that could work as Jimmy's room. Or Duncan said it was solid rock on the left side of the apartment, so they could add in over there. She'd have to ask him what his thoughts were.

"You okay?" Merri asked.

Marge nodded. She was so lost in thought that she had stopped in the middle of the sidewalk. "I was rearranging the apartment. The room Duncan was digging was supposed to be the new bedroom, but I started thinking that letting Jimmy have easy access to the caves was probably a bad idea, which led to rethinking the design."

"Yeah, that would be bad," Merri agreed. "My brothers used to get into all sorts of trouble when they were exploring the woods. I would think the caves would be just as bad to get lost in."

They walked for a few more minutes before the gates came into view. The lights were already on, and Merri punched in the code to open the side door. Marge could hear voices coming from the backyard and the smell of food on the grill. Her stomach rumbled, reminding her that she hadn't grabbed much for lunch. It was nice having family to come home to.

17

arge woke up, Duncan's warm body curled around her. She could feel his breath brushing against her hair, his arm firmly tucked around her waist, holding her close. Marge never would have guessed it by looking at him, but he was such a cuddler in his sleep. She had worried about sharing a bed with someone as it had always been just her, but it made her feel safe. Sometimes she would get a little overheated since his body naturally ran warmer and she would scoot a little bit away, but by morning he'd be spooning her again.

Feeling a little playful this morning, she rocked her hips back, rubbing her cheeks against his groin. He moaned a little in his sleep, his hips rocking up to meet hers, his dick starting to harden. She swiveled her hips in a small circle, his shaft now at full length against her back.

"Good morning to me," Duncan said, voice rough with sleep, his hand sliding up to cup her breast, gently thumbing the nipple.

"Hmm, morning," Marge replied. Duncan slung a leg over her hip, sliding it between her legs and hooking his foot around her ankle to open her legs. His hand slowly glided down her chest, skirting her belly button, which she appreciated since she was ticklish there, to slide into her panties. She spread her legs farther apart, giving him room. He unerringly found her clit, just barely touching it, teasing her. She tried to move her hips to get more pressure, but his leg locked over her hip, holding her in place.

"Not yet, babe. I'm in the mood to play and explore," Duncan told her.

Marge groaned as he slid a finger between her folds, teasing her entrance. She could feel herself getting wetter, but he only slid one finger in, gently thrusting.

"Come on, mate," she demanded.

"Nope, going to take my time. We're always in a hurry. We can take our time today," Duncan replied. Sam was taking Jimmy fishing, so they had all morning to themselves; he wanted to explore his mate's body, find all her hotspots, know what made her frantic, what made her buzz.

Duncan slid over top of her, his legs coming to rest on either side of her body. Marge tried to grab his cock, wanting to drive him crazy too. Duncan grabbed her hands, holding them above her head with one hand.

"Uh uh," he said, before leaning down to kiss her, his tongue tracing against the seam of her lips, encouraging her to open.

Marge opened her mouth, twirling her tongue around his. His free hand slid under her camisole, sliding it slowly upward, freeing her breasts. Her nipples pebbled, his head bending down to gently rake his teeth over the tips, so light she barely felt it. As he sucked a nipple into his mouth, his tongue twirling around it, he slid the cami over her head, stopping at her wrists. He sat up, quickly using both hands to wrap the silky fabric around her wrists, keeping them together.

"Hold them there for me, love," Duncan demanded, sliding back down her body, peppering kisses as he went.

Across her breasts, down her stomach, across her hips, her upper thighs. They all got little nips and kisses, everywhere but where she needed him. Her vagina clenched, wanting to be filled, already moist and ready for him, but he only moved down her leg, kissing her knee, skimming his fingers over her mons, before working his way down to kiss her ankle. As she whimpered, he switched to the other leg, starting at the ankle and working his way up.

"Duncan," she protested as he passed over her vagina again to kiss a breast. "I need you." She moved her hands, pushing his head back down to her groin.

"Hmm," he hummed against her clit. "I told you not to move your hands," he said. Duncan grabbed her wrists, holding them between her breasts. He moved down her body, his legs on either side of her calves, pausing above her cunt. She sighed in relief as he finally ran his tongue along her lips, just barely parting them. Her hips lifted, trying to force him deeper, but he moved his head back. "I'm going to savor you, stop trying to rush me."

Marge groaned, thumping her head back against the pillow. With his body over her lower legs, she was trapped by his weight, unable to spread her legs any wider. Duncan kept hold of her bound wrists with one hand. The fingertips of the other hand lightly trailed down her body before joining his mouth at her entrance. His work-roughened hands felt so good against her skin, he knew just how much pressure to use, his thumb dipping between her folds pressing down on her clit, rubbing slowly. She groaned as she watched him lap at her lips, his tongue stiffening to slide into her heat, licking and thrusting. Sparks of pleasure shot through her as he slid a finger inside, his tongue moving up to lick at her clit, his beard rasping against her skin. When a second finger joined in, she couldn't stop her hips from thrusting against his hand. Between the dual sensations of his fingers and tongue, she knew it wouldn't take much to send her flying.

"More, Duncan. Please. Let me come," she gasped. He crooked his finger, hitting her G-spot on the next thrust in and she screamed out her orgasm.

Duncan slowly removed his fingers, his tongue gently licking at her juices. "Come on mate, I want to make you come again."

"This time on your dick, please," she said, moving her hands to wrap around his head, trying to pull him up her body.

Duncan leaned back, fisting his cock as he looked at her. "You're so beautiful," he said, dropping down to give her a kiss.

He moved to kneel between her legs, dragging her hips closer as her legs wrapped around him. Marge wrapped her tied hands around his neck. "Fuck me," she snarled. "I want to feel you." She gasped as he surged into her, his girth stretching her, just short of painful, but he was filling her so completely, rubbing against her nerve endings in the most perfect way. She tightened around him, her body already rushing toward another orgasm.

"Hard please. I need to come again," she whispered against his ear, biting down on the lobe. She allowed her nails to change into her cat's, running them down his back as far as she could with them still tied together. Duncan's hips pistoned into her, the muscles in his chest and biceps bunching with the power behind his thrusts, his balls slapping against her taint. A bead of sweat dripped down his chest, her eyes following it. Surging up, she licked, groaning at the salty taste. Digging her heels into his back, she encouraged him to go faster.

"Yes, there. Mmhm. You feel so good," she babbled at him. Duncan reached down, gripping her hips, tilting them slightly. The next thrust had her seeing stars, her ears buzzing at the force of her orgasm. Turning her head, she bit down on his mating mark, claiming him again. As his blood hit her tongue, she felt the heat of his release fill her, his deep groan reverberating in the room.

He collapsed over her, catching himself on his elbows so he wouldn't crush her. "Love you. That was amazing," he grunted, breath heavy.

"It was," she purred. "The perfect way to start the day."

They lay there a few minutes, catching their breath before he pulled out of her body, leaving her feeling empty. Duncan unwrapped her wrists, rubbing them lightly. "All good?" he asked, concerned.

"It was perfect," she replied, sitting up to give him a light kiss.

Duncan grinned, picking her up and carrying her into the bathroom. Getting the water hot, he carried her into the shower and washed her body, gently massaging her head as he shampooed and conditioned her hair. She felt pampered.

Grabbing the loofa, she washed down his body, dropping it to rub his shoulders. It was nice to spend time like this with her mate.

18

"We finally got something on him," Marco said, a terrifying smile on his face, anger burning in his eyes.

"What happened?"

"Where's Jimmy?" Marco asked.

"He's upstairs playing a video game," Duncan replied. He thought the boy would probably fall asleep too. He had been yawning when he asked if he could go play.

"Good. I don't want him to hear this. I followed the scent trail of Jimmy's parents. They were in Maine. There is a whole compound there, all kinds of shifters, a couple of the females were pregnant. I waited until I could get his parents isolated from the others. They're both water shifters, different types, and they're not fated mates. Barry paid them to get pregnant, raise the kid for a bit, and then they sold him to Barry for more money. They were trying to have another kid. Everyone there is in this breeding program. Once they get pregnant, Barry moves them to a town somewhere else in the country. When the kid gets to be close to shifting age, or if they show unusual talents, Barry takes them back sooner."

"Like Jimmy being a TruthSpeaker," Marge murmured.

"Exactly. Once I had information from his parents, I went back to the group to get more answers. One person volunteered a tiny bit of information before someone shut him up. Barry's trying to get rare shifters, not necessarily the one-offs, the really rare ones, but any and all rare species he's trying to get under his control," Marco said.

"For what purpose?" Rolf asked.

"Don't know yet. I don't know if it stops at a breeding program or if he's experimenting in different ways. I tried every trick I knew, but no one else was talking. They might not even know themselves. But Jimmy's parents were approached because both their bloodlines frequently have had special gifts pop up. The thing is, when you mix two different species, you never know what you are going to get. I asked about the kids who were born without any special gifts or who were born as a regular type of paranormal. No one wanted to talk about those kids. I couldn't get an answer out of anyone."

"He could create his own army," Doc said, disgust in his voice. "If he wanted to spread his message and gain control of the Convocation, having powerful paranormals and especially ones with strong unique gifts would be a great way to do that. He's had the time to set this in motion. If he is collecting unique gifts and paranormals, there must be a plan. We need to make sure our wards can hold. What if he comes here?" he asked, a bit of fear bleeding into his voice.

Emma grabbed her mate by the face, her expression stern. "Look at me," she demanded. "Nothing is going to happen to you, or to Jimmy, or to any other paranormal here. The wards are strong. We have our bond links. If he came, we'd hide you."

Doc took a breath and nodded. Marge had never seen him afraid. Although the situation was horrible, she wasn't quite sure why he would be scared. They had faced difficult situations in the past. Heck, this past year had Sam, Rolf, and Ian all injured, so why would this time be different? Looking at Doc, Marge realized she didn't know much of his backstory or what his shifter side was.

"Up to you," Rolf said suddenly.

Marge was confused. No one had spoken or even used the Clan link.

Doc looked at his mate. "I have to believe we can trust everyone here," she said. "Fate brought us all together at this time for a reason. Maybe it's to help stop Barry."

He nodded and let out a deep sigh. "Let's all go in the library, and I'll tell you a story. This can't go past the people in this room, for everyone's sake. I need that pledge before I can tell you, since it would put lives in danger."

"You have my word," Marco said, a pulse of magic accompanying the words.

"Mine as well," Gage replied.

Shaye slipped out of the room into the kitchen, Tess following her. Marge followed everyone else into the library. Doc had a chest set up near the large table. She had never looked in it, since it held his personal items, but she had a feeling those were part of what they were going to talk about.

Shaye and Tess came in carrying some snacks and closed the door, Tess throwing a silencing spell across the room. Marge looked at her, eyebrow raised. There was already a ward over the house and another over the town. How much protection did they really need?

"Just to be safe," Tess replied with a shrug, before going over to sit on Sam.

Shaye walked over to give Doc a hug, and Marge could see the tension leave his body. "It'll be alright, Dad," Shaye told him, kissing him on the cheek.

"I don't even know where to begin," he said, looking around the room.

"Your origin story, duh," Ian said. "Start right before ye changed the first time."

Doc nodded, Emma slipping her hand into his. "My tribe moved around. A lot. Years before I was born, they left Greece to avoid hunters. It worked for a while, but eventually hunters made their way to this country as well. The tribe would have brief stops when someone was going to have a baby, but we would move again within a month or two. When enough of us were about shifting age, we stopped for a while. Tribe leader didn't want us stumbling across humans or hunters and accidently shifting near them.

"My parents weren't the best, always a little distant. It only got worse when I shifted the first time. They would have killed me or outcast me then, but I was underage, and it was against Tribe law. You see, my tribe was all unicorns. That was the dig site Gawain and Merri explored on their trip to Yellowstone. Thalia, the tribe's healer, took me in after that. She protected me, taught me about healing. When I reached the age of adult, the tribe attacked me, even my own parents. I think they would have killed me, but Thalia stepped in. She was an elder and to injure or kill her was a death sentence. She patched me up, packed me a bag, and helped me leave.

"I would go back every few years to see her. We had a meeting place. She would collect anything she thought would be useful and would pass it on when we met. One day she wasn't there, and I left before anyone else could spot me. Gawain and Merri found a packet she buried at our tree. There was a letter addressed to me," Doc said, pausing in his story.

"Have you gone through it yet?" Marco asked, his voice soft, almost gentle.

Doc shook his head. "No, not yet. I know it's silly, but it feels like once I look at her last things, then she's gone all over again."

"What made them want to kill you?" Duncan asked.

"I didn't shift into a unicorn. They didn't want any more

attention brought to themselves, even though we weren't allowed to shift outside of the village walls."

"What are you, Doc?"

"I'm an alicorn," he replied. He looked at Emma and she nodded.

"I have to apologize to you," he said, looking at Duncan and Marge. "I wasn't entirely truthful with you, but my animal takes a long time to trust."

"It's okay," Marge said. "That's a big secret to keep and I completely understand not wanting to put yourself or your mate at risk." If people hunted unicorns, she could only imagine how gleeful they would be to know an alicorn existed. A flying unicorn would be their dream come true.

"That's not all, though," Doc said, taking another deep breath. "I'm immortal, as far as we can tell. Part of what Thalia collected for me were old books, manuscripts, anything to do with rare shifters, unique gifts, or alicorns in general. It looks like it's a true immortality, not like the general kind where there is still a slight risk of death. Like the Fae.

"And I can share it."

Marge choked on her water. "What?" She looked around. The Clan clearly knew about it. Duncan looked shocked. But what surprised her was the lack of surprise on Marco's and Gage's faces. Doc hadn't told them, as he wanted an oath beforehand, so how had they known?

"My animal side wanted a Tribe of his own. We performed the ceremony to initiate that bond slash link, and also to share my immortality with the Clan. Emma and I didn't want to outlive our kids."

Marge sat there in shock.

"We're kind of a mess of interwoven bonds," Shaye jumped in. "We all have the mate bond with our mates, then there's the Nightwood Clan blood bond and its own telepathic link, and now we have a Tribe link with Doc's alicorn.

It's its own separate bond and link. It can get confusing with all the different pieces, but we can talk to everyone over either the Clan or Tribe links."

"We can also say the immortality thing works. I would hae been dead without it," Ian said. "The bullet hit my heart."

Berkley pulled Ian into his lap, holding him close, his nose buried in Ian's neck.

"It's a horrible time to say this, but if you are interested, my beast would like to include you in his Tribe," Doc offered. "I don't know how the immortality would work with Jimmy, but from what we read, it passes on to any children you would have. I don't know if Jimmy would stay this age, or age to maturity and then stop like the Fae do, or what would happen. We're still trying to find out, but it's hard to find anything specific."

Marge sat there stunned.

'I think we should take it,' Duncan said. 'We're already part of the Clan, being part of Doc's Tribe seems logical. They're our family. It would be nice to know how it would affect Jimmy though.'

'Maybe we can wait to have him do it until we know for sure, or he's old enough?' Marge replied.

"We would love to join, but until we know how it will affect Jimmy, maybe he should wait," Duncan replied.

"He'll be fine. He can join now," Gage said.

Marco grinned, but at least this one looked happy. He shoved a manilla envelope at them. "Take it. This is all the adoption paperwork you'll need. He's yours."

Marge blinked at him, staring. Say what? What had just happened? She needed to sit down. Oh wait, she was already sitting down.

"What?" Duncan asked. She could feel the excitement running through their bond.

"His parents were douchebags. They won't be a problem anymore. I had the paperwork drawn up and filed. It's completely real. He's yours now," Marco replied.

Marge had a suspicion that Marco meant that Jimmy's parents were now dead.

"How do you know he can join the Tribe now and not have aging issues?" Doc asked, looking hard at Gage.

"Hello, Anonymous38," Gage replied. "I'm Anonymous1."

"Holy shit," Doc muttered, sitting down hard in his chair.

19

I t was only three in the afternoon, but Marge decided it was five o'clock somewhere, as the saying went. Last night had blown her mind. She had no idea Doc was a rare shifter, much less what animal sides Marco and Gage had been hiding. She had been a paranormal all her life, and what had been revealed had rocked her world. She had a new appreciation and empathy for what Shaye must have felt like when she found out the paranormal world existed. If it was shocking to a Guardian of the Library, it had to be doubly so for someone who had been human. Pouring herself a glass of wine, she took a large swallow.

Apparently, there was a whole secret rare paranormal forum on the dark web, founded by Gage who went by Anonymous1. The forum was a place for them to share information and to ask questions, just like any other forum, but this one had magical wardings to stop hackers and hunters. Gage tried to help other rare paranormals as he found them, guiding them to the forum and sharing any knowledge he had. He was able to sense another rare paranormal and had been the one who sent Doc the information on being a true immortal and how to share it with his chosen family. Doc was the only alicorn in existence, he was immortal. Gage was older than dirt, and so was Marco. Although Marco was about Doc's age. Which was also very old.

Marco was Gage's half-brother and had turned into a gargoyle right there in the library. He had been amazing to look at. Gage then shifted into a damned griffin, another shifter thought to be a myth. She had no idea how he got to be a Warden without anyone knowing about his animal side. The brothers had kept Gage's animal a secret from everyone. Their mother had died protecting them from hunters, which is what spurred them both to become Wardens when they were adults. Their fathers had never been in the picture. They were both immortal, Marco because Gage had done the same sharing ritual when they were children. Although gargoyles were in very small numbers, they weren't one of the one-offs and didn't have true immortality, just the normal immortality people associated with dragons and Fae. If an injury was bad enough, like a shot to the heart, or decapitation, they could still die. Whenever Marco had been injured on the job, the Convocation members assumed he healed because of his species version of immortality. It was easy enough to let everyone assume they were the same type of shifter. It made sense, most siblings were the same species.

After encouraging Doc to look through Thalia's packet to see if there was anything new, the brothers had left. Emma sent each of them home with a container of dinner and dessert, letting them know they were part of this family.

They were going to talk to Jimmy after dinner and let him know they had adopted him, as well as bring up joining the Clan and Doc's Tribe. If he didn't want to join now, they would make sure he knew he could always join at a later time. He was out on a nature hike with Doc, who was showing him beneficial plants. The kid was going to be incredibly well rounded in his education. Duncan was working with Sam, Rolf, and Berkley at the apartment today, working on the expansion. They had talked and drawn up some new plans. They were adding two new rooms and a bathroom to the left side of the living room. One of those rooms would be Jimmy's bedroom. For now, the other room would be used for storage. It was easier to build it out at the same time as the other rooms. She already had an office upstairs and Rolf had contractors building a workshop for Duncan on the Clan's estate. They had both agreed that they needed a door to the caves. Duncan had framed out a wall and installed a door. If you stood in the living room, it looked like any other room. They planned on keeping it locked to discourage a curious little boy from exploring. The library and their bedroom would be switching places. It would make for a better layout, and they would be closer to Jimmy's room if he had a nightmare. They had picked out a new loveseat to match the couch that was already in the living room. It would ensure that they could each have a seat, plus there would be room for a few guests. The kitchen and laundry would stay on the right side of the main room. She'd had to move some bookcases around, but she thought the final result would be worth it. As a surprise for Duncan, she had a large screen TV ordered; she mainly read or watched on her phone or tablet and didn't have a television.

She felt a hand on her arm, calm spreading through her. She turned her head, finding Shaye standing next to her.

"You okay?" Shaye asked, concern on her face.

Marge nodded. "It's just a lot. I went from having a friend I didn't spend a lot of time with in Gage, to being drawn into this group, kidnapped, finding my mate, joining the Clan, adopting a kid. And now I find out that my oldest friend is a rare paranormal, so is Doc. Barry, who should be protecting paranormals as part of the Convocation, is part of some weird hunter group that is kidnapping paranormals, as well as breeding others for kids for some unknown reason. How are you not running off screaming into the woods right now?" Marge asked. "You only found out about paranormals a year ago, found your mate, had your father-in-law try to kill him multiple times, turned, took part in the fight that got rid of Vlad, plus all the other things that happened to this family. I've always been a shifter, and I feel overwhelmed."

Shaye laughed, grabbing the bottle of wine to pour herself a glass. "That does sound tempting some days." She took a sip, thinking. "The mate bond helps. I can feel his feelings for me, even more since we mated. My two best friends joined me here, and now I have this amazing family surrounding me. Emma is like everyone's mom, and she is my mother-in-law at this point. Doc is a great father figure. I grew up thinking I was unwanted, knowing I was unloved. At least by my birth family. Tess and Ian kept me together when it got rough. This, here with everyone, is what I've always wanted. I'm going to do my best to protect it, although I'm better at healing than I am at fighting," she said with a grin.

"I don't know. I've heard stories of the battle against Vlad," Marge said, raising her glass in a toast, grinning as she saw Shaye blush.

"Shush. Anyway, maybe we can have a scream-in-the-woods night this weekend before the run."

"Sounds like a plan," Marge said, gently bumping her shoulder against Shaye's.

"Did you hear back from the school advisor yet?"

"I think tomorrow is when they're supposed to call. On one hand, I want him to get in because he wants it so badly. But on the other hand, I was selfishly looking forward to him hanging out with me at the library some days."

"If he does get in, he can always hang out with you after school. It's not that far of a walk," Shaye pointed out.

"That's true," Marge acknowledged. "He could work on homework or whatever."

"And if you're working late, there's enough of us working

in town that can bring him back to the Clan house, at least until your apartment is done."

"Is Rolf really okay with us living at the library?" Marge asked. They had just joined the Clan and would soon be joining Doc's Tribe, but once the library apartment was finished, they were planning on moving back there.

Shaye nodded. "He just wants everyone to be happy. Ian and Berkley still have some space above the shop, and I think they added a small bedroom to their workshop. Emma and Doc have his house in town, Sam has the apartment at the brewery. Gawain has his RV. Everyone has a separate space they can go to. Just because you want to live at the library, doesn't mean you aren't part of this family. We all understand you're the Guardian and would feel more comfortable being there. Plus, there are wards on the library and all around the town now, so you'll be safe."

"Face it, you're stuck with us," Tess laughed as she came in carrying multiple bags. "I grabbed dinner on the way home from the Chinese place. Everyone is about five minutes out, although the guys will probably need to grab a shower."

"I'll call Albert and have them come back," Emma said as she walked in from the backyard. She had been reading on the outdoor couch.

"How was the clinic today?" Shaye asked Tess.

Marge got up and helped Emma pull out plates, silver-ware, and cups for everyone. It was nice feeling like she was part of this family.

Minutes later she was groaning as she saw Jimmy standing on the back deck with Doc. They both had huge grins on their faces, their clothes covered in mud with bits of twigs and leaves sticking to them. Emma laughed.

"We can always hose them off outside," Emma suggested.

"That's not a bad idea. It's hot enough out that they won't be cold. I don't want him tracking the mud throughout the house."

"I'll run upstairs and get towels. Once they're rinsed off, they can leave their clothes out there and wrap up in a towel," Emma suggested.

Marge nodded. She stepped outside to cut them off before they made it to the back door.

"It looks like you guys had fun," she said, eyeing them. They looked even dirtier up close. Doc's normally white hair was tinged with brown. What in the world had they gotten into?

"It was so much fun. We slid into the creek and found some tadpoles. There's all kinds of plants. There's one that grows next to poison ivy, but it helps you not itch from the poison ivy oils. There's some that act like a pain reliever, some you can even eat. We found wild berries!"

"That does sound fun," Marge agreed. "I think we're going to have you take your boots off and we're going to hose you down out here, so you don't get mud all over the house."

"That's probably a good plan," Doc agreed, leading the way to the hose reel. He sprayed himself down first, stripping down to his boxer-briefs. Marge was a little surprised to see Doc was cut, his abdomen taunt with a six-pack. She never would have thought he would be so muscular. Not as handsome as her Duncan though.

Emma brought out the towels, and Doc handed Jimmy the hose, reaching for a towel to dry off with.

Jimmy started washing himself, starting with his hair. "It'd probably work better if you got down to your underwear like Doc did," Marge said, watching the muddy clothes stick to him. They'd be here all night trying to rinse the mud off his body if he left the clothes on. She shouted when he suddenly disappeared, a pile of clothes left behind.

"What the—?" Doc startled. He rushed over, turning the hose off, looking around for the boy.

Marge ran toward the clothes, sniffing, trying to find a

trace of her boy. The water was muting the scents. She didn't even notice the tears running down her face.

"Jimmy! Where are you?" she yelled. "The wards wouldn't let him be taken, would they?"

Emma shook her head, her phone out, calling Rolf. "No. They keep ill intentions out, even spells. There's no way a kidnapping wouldn't be considered ill intentioned. Rolf," she said as he answered. "Jimmy was rinsing off with the hose and disappeared. Where are you?"

Marge stopped listening, stripping down to shift into her cat. She would have better smell in this form. Her whiskers twitched as her nose scented the bundle of clothes, moving them out of the way.

Duncan came running around the side of the house. "What happened?" He stopped suddenly, seeing his mate in her cat form. She walked toward him, something in her mouth.

"What is it?" he asked. Opening his hands, she walked over to him, gently placing a small body in his hands. She took a step back, shifting back to human and throwing her clothes back on, not even noticing that her entire family had just seen her naked.

"It's Jimmy. He shifted," she said, running a hand down the sleek fur.

Duncan held his hands up, peering into the little eyes, seeing his son look back at him. "Well, hello there. We weren't expecting this quite yet," he told him.

Jimmy squeaked in response, his little nose twitching as he took in all the new smells.

"So, he's an otter?" Duncan asked.

Marge nodded. "A river otter. He can go playing in the creek, maybe even the pool in the cave if the water's safe for him."

Duncan put him down on the ground, letting him explore.

Jimmy looked toward the backyard, and then back to everyone else. "You want to go on a run?" he guessed.

The little otter nodded.

Marge shifted back to her cat, Sam, Gawain, and Doc shifting to their forms. She looked at her mate, tilting her head in question.

"I'm too big to run through the woods, I'll stay human for now and I'll run that way," Duncan said.

Marge rubbed her head against his leg, leading the little otter on a slow walk through the yard, letting him get used to his animal form.

"He's adorable," Shaye said quietly.

"He is," Duncan agreed. "He probably won't be shifted long, and he'll be tired and hungry when he shifts back. The first time always takes a lot out of them."

"Dinner's ready, I just put it in the oven to keep warm. Good thing I ordered extra," Tess said. "I bet Rolf puts a pool in for next summer."

Shaye nodded. "Probably. Go run with them, we'll stay here, grab some extra clothes for him, and get the table ready for dinner. That way he can eat and go straight to bed if he's really tired."

"Thank you," Duncan said before running to catch up with his family.

20

Marge grunted as a finger poked her nose. Cracking her eyes open, she saw Jimmy standing next to the bed.

"Morning," she said, rubbing the sleep out of her eyes. "What's up? Are you okay?"

He bit his lip but nodded. "We were supposed to talk last night, but then I shifted and fell asleep at dinner. I'm sorry. What did you want to talk to me about?"

Marge shook Duncan awake. Sitting up, she gestured Jimmy to climb on the bed. "We had a couple of things to talk about, but some of them have to wait until everyone is up."

"Okay," he said, drawing out the word a little. She could hear the faintest hints of preteen attitude in the word.

"Gage and Marco found out some things about your parents. They were working with Barry and gave you to him. Your school wasn't really at fault for letting them take you. Marco found some lingering evidence that the school secretary had her memories altered."

Jimmy nodded. "Are they still alive? Do I have to go with them?"

Marge looked at Duncan, who gave a tiny nod. They

maybe didn't have to go into a lot of details today, and they didn't even know the whole story behind how his parents died, although they could guess. "You do not have to go back. They're not alive any longer. Even if they were, since they were working with Barry, we wouldn't let them have you. Marco drew up the papers, and because we talked about it before, we adopted you. No one can take you away," she reassured him.

"Really?" he asked, hope written all across his face.

"Yup," Duncan said. "Go get dressed and we can get breakfast started for everyone. Then we can talk about the rest of the things when everyone is up."

The boy jumped up, grabbing them both in hugs. "Thank you," he said, his voice a little choked with tears that he wouldn't let fall. "I'll go get ready," he said, running out of the room.

Marge stretched, her shirt riding up to show her stomach. "Hm, I was hoping we would get to sleep in today," she grumbled quietly.

Duncan reached out, lightly tracing a finger over her exposed skin. "I'd love to stay in bed with you, but I have a feeling that he'll be back in a couple minutes. I'll grab a quick shower and have him help me make pancakes. I think he should be able to make those pretty easily. You can take your time getting ready," he said, bending down to give her a quick kiss.

Marge grinned. "I want a better kiss before you leave the room. After I brush my teeth," she said. She had very firm opinions on kissing with morning breath. As in, don't do it.

Duncan kissed her forehead and walked to the bathroom. She heard the toilet flush, the sink turned on, and then the shower. She wanted a shower too, so she would be a little later downstairs, but she didn't want to miss their first making breakfast together as an official family. She had a feeling once the smell of bacon rose throughout the house, everyone else would trickle downstairs. Letting herself have one more large stretch, she got up and threw the covers over the bed. Leaning against the counter, she admired the view of her mate showering while she brushed her teeth. Rinsing out her mouth, she gently closed the bathroom door before she slowly crept toward the shower. Grabbing the door, she gingerly opened it, making sure he didn't hear her. With his back facing her as he washed his hair, she slid a hand between his legs, running her fingertips over his sac.

"Ah!" Duncan screamed.

Marge fell back laughing. "What was that? Is my big bad dragon afraid of something?"

"It's my balls! Of course I'm afraid of things unexpectedly touching them," he protested.

"Let me make it up to you," Marge said as she dropped her clothes into the hamper, climbing into the shower stall with him. Luckily, Rolf had designed the house with over-sized bathrooms and the showers were no different. They both fit easily. Dropping to her knees, she pushed Duncan until he was blocking the flow of water from hitting her face. Leaning in, she nuzzled his groin, his penis already filling. Licking a path from the base of his balls to the tip of his dick, his shaft was fully hard by the time she was done.

"Hm, I like this way of making it up to me, but we don't have much time," he said, his hand coming down to cup her cheek.

"I'll be quick." She grinned at him. Without any other warning, she slammed down on him, her mouth and throat engulfing him as she deep throated his hard length. She had been getting better at taking him deeper and she kept him in her throat, swallowing around him until she needed a breath. Marge slid her hand up his inner thigh, coming to cup his testicles. They were already drawn up tight. She brushed them gently with her fingertips, her other hand coming around to grab his butt, pulling him in closer. She pulled out all the things she knew drove him wild, trying to make sure he came before there was a knock on the door. Just as his hips started speeding up, a voice called out from the other room.

"I'm ready! Where are you?"

"In the bathroom. I'll be out of the shower in a minute. Why don't you read, and I'll come get you when I'm done," Duncan choked out, gripping her head as he came in her mouth.

Marge swallowed his release. Giving the head of his cock one last gentle kiss, she stood. "Better go get dressed. I'll be down in a few minutes," she said, giving him a kiss.

"Thank you, babe," Duncan said, kissing her deeply before sliding out of the shower.

She heard the bedroom door shut and hurried through the rest of her shower and shaving routine. Fifteen minutes later, she was standing in the kitchen, watching Duncan show Jimmy how to make pancakes, the smell of bacon already coming from the oven. She had never thought she would have kids, but this sight was making her think that maybe one day they could give Jimmy a sibling. She was sure he would make friends at school, but it would be nice if he had some siblings or cousins to play with. This was a family, whether or not they shared blood, and any babies that came along would be his family as well. And if he chose to take Doc's offer, he would be immortal. Having other people closer to his age would be good for him.

"Do we have chocolate chips or blueberries?" she asked, making her presence known. She was pretty sure Duncan had already known she was there.

"Chocolate chip pancakes?" Jimmy asked. "I saw some in the pantry. I'll go get them." He rushed off, leaving Marge and Duncan standing there.

Duncan nodded toward the coffee pot. "It's just about done brewing. I got the caramel syrup you like, but I forgot to buy whipped cream. I was going to top his pancakes with some."

"He'll still like it with chocolate chips," she reassured him.

"I have heavy cream in the fridge," Emma said, coming into the room. "I can make some whipped cream," she offered.

"Whipped cream and chocolate chips! This is the best day ever!" Jimmy shouted, running back with the chocolate chips.

Doc laughed as he came in. "Just don't get too used to it. You still have to eat healthy most of the time," he said, ruffling Jimmy's hair.

"I know."

Doc looked at Marge and Duncan, tilting his head toward the boy.

"We thought we could finish our talk over breakfast," Duncan said. "We told him about the adoption, so this is a bit of a celebration breakfast. We wanted to wait until everyone else was here to have the other conversation."

"A celebration breakfast sounds perfect," Doc replied.

Marge watched as Jimmy concentrated intently on flipping the pancake. The tip of his tongue was sticking out between his lips while he was trying to scoop up the pancake without breaking it. He quickly flipped it, and it landed mostly on the griddle, only a little bit overlapping with another pancake. Duncan helped him guide the pancake into place. It didn't take them long to achieve a nice stack. When the timer went off, Marge pulled the bacon out of the oven and placed it on some paper towels to drain. Emma took some leftover muffins from the day before out of the fridge, as well as the butter and maple syrup. Within a couple of minutes, everyone was downstairs, the kitchen filling with the sounds of conversation and laughter.

Marge took a bite of the fluffy pancake, loving how Duncan had given her blueberry ones, knowing they were her favorite. She moaned a little as it hit her tongue, the perfect pancake bite. They must have all been hungry because the table got a lot quieter once they all sat down with food. When everyone was finished eating and just sipping on their coffees, she looked at Jimmy.

"You know how we said we had other things to talk about and that everyone had to be here? Rolf and Doc wanted to talk to you," she said.

Rolf cleared his throat. "We wanted to know if you wanted to join the Cl—" he started to ask.

"Yes!" Jimmy said, jumping out of his chair. "Yes, yes, yes. I want to be part of the family too."

"Hold on," Rolf said, laughing. "You're a part of this family either way. There are a few things you need to know first. And they're things you can't talk to anyone else about, other than us, Gage, and Marco. It's to keep everyone here safe, including you. Okay?"

Jimmy nodded, his hair bouncing with the force of his nods.

"We're a Clan, but we're a little closer than most Clans are. When Sam was hurt, the only way to save him was to do a blood bond. Do you know what that is?"

Jimmy shook his head.

"It's pretty rare anymore. Most of us hadn't heard of it before either. You would pledge to follow the Clan leader, me. I would need to bite you. Once we do that, you'll have the same telepathic link that the rest of us do to each other. It's forever though; it's not a bond that can be easily broken."

"Does it hurt?"

"Maybe for a second or two," Shaye said. "But I'm here and can heal it right up so it doesn't hurt longer."

"Okay, let's do this," Jimmy said resolutely.

"Well. We're not done quite yet. This is the big one. You need to think about this one very carefully, okay?" Rolf said.

Once Jimmy nodded, Doc spoke up. "I'm a very rare shifter. I'm the only one of my kind. My animal claimed everyone here, besides you, Marge, and Duncan as his Tribe. He'd like to have you as part of his Tribe as well, but there are some consequences to it. I'm immortal, like really truly immortal. You know how the Fae and even dragons like Duncan are considered immortal? They can still die though; it takes a lot and has to be a catastrophic injury like injuring their heart, but they can be hurt enough to die. It just doesn't happen very often. Mine isn't like that. It's really immortal, you can have a huge injury and it might take a while to heal, but you won't die. If you have your own kids when you grow up, they would be immortal too."

"I'd be stuck as a kid forever?" he asked, horrified.

"No, no. You'd still grow until a certain age and then stop. I'm not sure what age that would be, but it would be when you're considered an adult."

"You wouldn't be able to tell anyone about Doc's shifter side or the immortality thing," Duncan cautioned.

"Because Barry would try to take him," Jimmy said. "He can't have you. You're ours," he growled, his shifter side coming out a little bit.

"Right. Think about it and see what you want to do. You don't have to decide now," Marge said.

"Like Rolf said, you're already part of this family, so we wanted you to have this," Berkley said, putting a pendant around Jimmy's neck. "It glows when danger is nearby, but only we can see it glow. It will shift with you, so you don't need to take it off. It's also spelled to protect you against evil intentions and to conceal your paranormal status from human hunters." They had decided to wait until now to give him his pendant. He was in the house or on the grounds with one of them at all times, so he wasn't in danger. Now though, he may be starting school and even with the town wards, they wanted to be careful. The main reason they waited until today though was if he wanted to take time to decide on joining, they wanted him to still feel like part of the family.

"I want to join everything. When can we do it?"

Rolf looked at Doc, who shrugged.

"We can do the Clan one right now, but Doc needs some time to set up his. Do you want to take care of the Clan oath while he gets ready?" Rolf asked.

"Yes, please."

Marge watched as Rolf initiated the telepathic link. Jimmy flinched a little at the bite, but Marge could tell Rolf was trying to be as gentle as possible. Once Rolf let go, Shaye placed her hand on Jimmy's back, and the wounds healed instantly.

'Can you hear me?' he shouted.

Everyone winced.

'Yes, we can, but you don't need to shout,' Duncan told him.

"Try saying something just to me," Marge encouraged him. "You have to focus and find the thread that goes to each person. Concentrate on that and try to say something to only them."

'Like this?' he asked, his face all scrunched up in concentration.

Marge looked around. She didn't think anyone else had heard. "Did you guys hear him?"

"Just like that! Good job!" she praised after getting head shakes from everyone.

Emma came into the room from the kitchen. "Albert's ready."

The whole family traipsed back into the kitchen, where Doc explained what the ritual was.

His nose wrinkled, but Jimmy drank his bit down, followed by Marge and Duncan. She felt a whole-body tingle. It was quite pleasant and left her feeling almost euphoric.

'Mine?' a new voice said.

"That's Albert's animal," Emma explained. "He's a bit different than other shifters; they're more of a separate entity."

'Hi!' Jimmy shouted again. *'Oops. Sorry, too loud. Hi! Did it work?'* he asked quieter.

Doc nodded. "It did. Welcome to the Clan and the Tribe."

"How about we go hang out in the backyard for a bit?" Sam asked. "I can finish showing you how to whittle."

"Yes! Let's go!" He ran out of the room, leaving the back door open, Rockefeller following him out.

"Marge, can you or Duncan bring Jimmy into the clinic sometime this week? Marco got his immunization records from the school and he's missing a couple that he needs before school starts," Doc said.

"Yeah, one of us will be able to bring him in. Would Wednesday work? I have the summer reading program wrap-up on Monday and Tuesday," she replied.

"Wednesday is great. Tess is in the office that day as well, so Shaye can help with the shots."

Marge looked at him, a question on her face.

'Just in case he has a reaction. Either emotional or physical. His medical record was very spotty in the school file, so I'm not sure how accurate it was. Plus, I don't know what Barry did to him while he had him,' Doc explained silently.

'That makes sense. I'll see if Merri can watch the desk for an hour or so and I'll bring him over Wednesday. Let me know when is a good time,' Marge replied. She watched as Ian handed Jimmy a leather apron to wear while whittling, the size a little large, but it was covering any area where he might slip and cut himself. Sam readjusted the way he was holding the knife and the piece of wood. Duncan slipped behind her, wrapping an arm around her stomach as they watched him laugh and have fun.

21

Marge looked down at her phone, checking the time again. Jimmy was at his first day of school. The school had a staggered start; the first day being only for new students. It let them explore the school, figure out where their lockers and classrooms were, how the lunch line worked, all that fun stuff you had to learn at a new place. Berkley and Gage had created a spell that would cause his pendant to change temperature when he started to access his TruthSpeak powers. They didn't want to block his use of powers in the unlikely event that he would need them, but they wanted him to be aware of when he might accidently pull on them and could stop himself. Today was a half day and she didn't want to be late picking him up from school. Merri was taking over while she was gone, but Jimmy would be coming back to the library to work on any school work he had and to hang out with her until closing. Sam had promised to drop off a lunch for him when they returned.

So far it had gone pretty smoothly. The vaccines hadn't caused any issues, Shaye being there to help him feel better afterward. It had been fun going school supply shopping. She had no idea there were so many notebook options, much less pencil cases. He had things he was excited to use and had painstakingly written his name on all of his things like the teacher letter had instructed. The school had assured them that if they ran into something he was behind in, they would have a tutor to assist at school. Emma also said she would work with him on anything he needed. She had done an amazing job getting him caught up.

Merri came over, walking behind the desk to gently push her out of the way. "You've checked your phone about twenty times now. It's close enough. Start walking to school and get him. I'll let Sam know to get started on his lunch, so he doesn't have to wait long to eat. It's quiet here, now go."

Marge laughed. "I'm going. Duncan is supposed to meet me there. He was at the Clan house this morning talking with the contractors about his warehouse/workshop."

"I can't wait to see some of his pieces. The pictures he had looked amazing," Merri said.

"Me too," Marge agreed. Although she was eager to see him work. His dragon was gorgeous, but huge and she was curious to see how such a big body could create smaller sculptures.

Leaving the library, she took a deep breath, calming her own nerves. She didn't want Jimmy to pick up on her nervousness; she just really wanted his day to have gone well.

She stood outside the school in the pick-up area, Duncan arriving only a minute or so after her. "Were you nervous too?" he asked, wrapping an arm around her waist.

Marge nodded. "Merri kicked me out," she said with a laugh. "How did the meeting go?"

"Good. They think they can get it done by the end of September. I have pretty minimal needs, so it should go quickly. They can tap into the power, sewer, and water lines they had to run for Ian and Berkley's workshop, so that will make it easier."

"I can't wait to see you work," Marge told him.

"My storage container should be arriving next week. Some of my unsold pieces are in there, along with my equipment. I had a few customers reach out to ask about custom pieces; it'll be good to get back to work," Duncan said.

"Are you going to try to get a display store in town?"

"I'm going to focus on online orders for a while, I think. Ian and Berkley offered the area behind their shop to meet customers and to keep a few pieces. They have a nice little garden back there. We'll see how it goes. I've never had my own shop before; I like creating things, not really the selling and storefront type of stuff."

Rolf had already told him that if a building came up for sale and he liked it, to let him know. Just like the museum and Gawain, Rolf would buy it for him. He had even heard Rolf on the phone with his realtor telling her to keep an eye open for property that went up for sale near his land. Duncan supposed that between the workshops and the large garage that had recently been built, Rolf wanted to keep a lot of area for runs. Not that they were running out of space, but he could see where looking forward was beneficial.

Speaking of, "Are you looking forward to the museum opening?" he asked. It was due to officially open next weekend. Sam was creating an hors d'oeuvres menu and everyone had taken the day off. They would be working in shifts, although he thought Merri and Gawain were planning on being there all day.

"I am. I saw it when it was being set up, and then I saw it briefly when I brought Steve and Marshall over. Merri was going to have an early open house for just us once she finished getting it all ready. She had a few last-minute things to do."

"I've seen bits and pieces when Gawain asked for help or opinions. I'm curious to see how it all comes together," he said.

They heard a bell sound inside the school, a teacher

coming out seconds later, opening the front doors.

Jimmy came bounding down the stairs, a smile on his face. "That was awesome!" he shouted, running up to them.

"You had a good day then?" Marge asked.

Jimmy grabbed their hands as he walked between them, surprising them. "I did. My teacher's really nice. They have a cool lunchroom, and they have hot lunch every day. Can I buy sometimes? I made a new friend. He's a year older, but he's really nice. His parents moved here a while ago, but he was homeschooled. He wanted to make friends too, so he came to school."

"What's his name?" Marge asked. She knew all the kids in town and would at least know if it was one of the nicer kids or not, and if he was a paranormal or human. There weren't too many paranormal kids in town though.

"Dave."

"Dave Youger?" she asked, thinking of boys who would be a year older than him.

"I think that was it," Jimmy said, shrugging.

"If it is, you're right. He's a nice kid." And a witch. His parents worked at the National Park, which fit them well as they had an affinity for plants and animals. Dave had been homeschooled because he had problems controlling his powers when he was younger, creating flowers in the middle of winter, talking to the squirrels, that kind of thing. Nothing that would hurt anyone, but something that humans would have thought was weird. Marge thought his parents were probably more comfortable having him go to school now that the town knew there were paranormals and there were wards over the town to protect it. They didn't have to worry as much about him being hurt for accidently revealing his powers now.

"I know his parents work late some days, so you can always invite him to hang out with you in the library, if you want," Marge offered.

"Thanks!" he said. "Can we get something to eat? I'm getting hungry."

"Sam is bringing you over lunch," Marge replied.

"Cool."

The short walk back to the library was filled with little stories and information about his school day. She exchanged a glance with Duncan, both of them happy that he had such a good experience. Of course, tomorrow would probably be a little more stressful since the whole school was going to be there, but at least now he would be more comfortable with the space and knew someone.

Sam had dropped off the lunch, along with a surprise lunch for her, Duncan, and Merri. He had included a couple of cookies in Jimmy's box, which delighted him to no end. After they ate, Jimmy explored the library for a little bit. Duncan took him downstairs to see the work on the apartment. He had been excited to help pick out paint colors and furniture for his room.

Both of their phones buzzed, Merri grabbing hers first. "Doc's calling an all-family meeting tonight. Gage is on the group chat too."

"Does it say what for?" Marge asked, alarmed. Sundays were kept as a family day, but otherwise there weren't all-family meetings called except for emergencies.

Merri shook her head. "That was it," she said. "I'm going to order some pizzas. I'll grab them on the way home. That way no one has to worry about dinner on top of whatever is going on."

The front door of the library opened, and Marge schooled her face back into a welcoming look, not the alarmed one she was sure had been there.

"Ian! Do you know what's going on?" Merri asked, holding up her phone.

"Nae. We got the same message and then nothing. I called Rolf, who said Doc was fine earlier. Doc was holed up in the library, so Rolf didnae ken anything else. I guess he had taken the day off work today. The girls were at the clinic, treating minor things. I hae no idea what's going on. I stopped by Sam's and he didnae ken either. He's leaving early and putting one of the supervisors in charge for the night. Gage wasn't in his office when I stopped by."

"I'm going to grab pizzas for dinner," Merri said, "so I may be a few minutes later than normal."

"Sounds good. I'm going to head back and help Berkley close up. See ye at home," Ian said.

Marge looked at Merri, who shrugged. "I have no idea."

'What's with the message?' Duncan asked.

'No idea. Ian was just in here. Neither he, Berkley, or Sam know what's going on. Gage isn't in the office. Merri's picking up pizza for dinner. I'm not sure what tonight's going to look like,' she replied.

'Huh. Okay then. Everything seemed fine when I left this afternoon,' Duncan said.

They worked to close the library in a hurry. If they didn't get all the books put away, well it would just have to wait until tomorrow.

Gawain met Merri outside the library, and they walked down to the pizza place. It seemed like everyone was on edge. Looking down the street, the clinic and the Winged Potter looked closed up for the night.

"What's going on?" Jimmy asked. "Are my parents really not dead? Is Barry trying to get me?"

"What? No!" Marge exclaimed. She hadn't even realized he had picked up on everyone's worry and internalized it.

"Doc called a meeting, which he normally doesn't do. Your parents are dead," Duncan reassured him. "Marco told us so, and he wouldn't lie to us. If anything was a danger to you, he or Gage would let us know first. Okay? I don't know what's going on, but it isn't about you."

Jimmy nodded, but he was still quiet the rest of the way

home. Shaye met them at the door, pulling Jimmy into a hug. Marge watched as the tension left his little body. "You're safe. No one's going to take you away," she heard Shaye murmur to him. Marge was incredibly grateful Shaye had the ability to soothe as well as heal.

Merri and Gawain came in minutes later. Ian and Berkely were already in the kitchen getting plates and drinks out. They hadn't seen Doc or Emma yet. When there was a knock on the door, Duncan walked over to open it, finding both Gage and Marco there.

"What's going on?" Gage asked quietly.

"No one knows. Doc is still in the library. We have pizza though," he offered with a half-hearted grin. He had a feeling that whatever they heard would leave them with little appetite, so maybe they should eat beforehand. Although cold pizza was good too.

Emma came out of the library, her eyes red. Rolf ran to her, "You okay?" he asked, grabbing his mom in a hug.

Emma nodded. "Everyone grab some food and come into the library. Albert finally went through Talia's package for him. It's—" She stopped, swallowing. "Albert can tell you," she said, her eyes tearing up.

The mood was somber, everyone grabbing a slice of pizza. Emma grabbed one for her and Doc as well. When they entered the library, Doc was slumped over, resting his head on the table. The entire surface was covered in papers and notes, the fur that had been covering the package lay on a chair off to the side. He had even pulled out a folding table to have more room.

"Eat. I'll get to this in a minute," Doc said. Looking over at Jimmy, he asked, "Did you have a good first day of school?" Marge could tell he was trying to keep things as normal as possible for the boy.

Jimmy nodded. "It was fun. I made a new friend, Dave."

"Youger?" Doc asked.

"Yup," he replied.

"He's a good kid. I've known him for about ten years, since his parents moved here," Doc replied. "I think he'll make a great friend."

After that, it fell silent, everyone focusing on eating and not sure what to say.

"Would you like to come to the kitchen with me and get some ice cream?" Emma asked Jimmy.

He looked around the room, stopping on Marge. "Do I have to?" he asked quietly.

Doc spoke up then. "Jimmy, I promise this doesn't have to do with your parents or you. Not directly. There are some things I found that are awful and horrible that you don't need to hear or see. Marge and Duncan can tell you the basics afterward. We're never going to lie to you or keep you out of something, but this isn't something you should have to deal with at your age. You've seen enough bad things; we don't want to be the cause of you seeing more."

Jimmy nodded. "Okay," he said, giving Emma a hug. Marge thought it was his way of apologizing for implying he didn't want to go with her at first.

Doc waited until the door shut. "I think I know what Barry's been up to, but it started long before he was born. If I'm right, which is where Gawain's and Merri's research skills are going to come in handy to confirm it, it started before him. For sure his father was involved, I'm not clear if it was his grandfather too, or if it started with his dad."

"What did you find?" Gage asked.

"They're collecting certain types of paranormals. I think they're kidnapping them and forming their own type of zoo. Maybe even a forced breeding program," Doc said.

Well, crap. She hadn't seen that one coming.

22

"What?" rang out loudly in the room from just about everyone.

"Thalia had records of paranormals even I haven't heard of. Some of the ones on the list are still around, although their numbers are small. Like gargoyles," he said, looking at Marco. "Some are ones I had thought were extinct or myths, like jackalopes. Others are clearly the one-offs, the rare ones like Gage and me. I don't know why she started keeping track of some, maybe it was to try to show me others I could try to connect with who would understand where I was coming from and the need for secrecy, I don't know. But she kept records of the ones she met or heard about. One by one, they seemed to dwindle in numbers or disappear altogether. She heard rumors from passing paranormals about disappearances. People who had neighbors or friends who were suddenly gone one day. Now, back then, communication was harder. Heck, life was harder. People died, and people didn't notice or even get the news of it for months sometimes. When she started digging into it more, even sneaking out to go to other settlements, there was a pattern, much like Daryl said with his family's neighbors. Someone in power showed up. Days later, people were gone.

"She collected records, getting statements from other people. She started forming a little network of people she trusted who had been noticing odd things as well. They sent each other messages and updates. She met a hydra shifter during one of these outings. They told her they felt watched, some weird vampire guy from the Convocation approached them asking all sorts of intrusive questions. They didn't feel safe, so they gave her a book that they had had in their family for years. Their family were record keepers, historians. They had worked for the Convocation since it began, but their uncle came home one day and forced them all to leave. He said it wasn't safe anymore and he took the book with him. The hydra Thalia met was a child when it happened and eventually became the guardian of the book. This book," he said, holding up the ancient-looking text. Marge could tell it was extremely old and there was a very faint preservation spell still on it, although it was almost out of power. "This book lists every known paranormal at the time it was written, about five hundred years before I was born. It even marks which ones are true immortals. There used to be a lot more of us," he said to Gage. "While the uncle never disclosed what had scared him, at least not that this person knew about, they said their family still maintained the book and kept an ear out for Convocation business. They heard whispers about a collector, someone who only wanted rare paranormals or rare gifts.

"They had a selkie friend who could turn any water into ice with just a thought. They had plans together and when they didn't show, the hydra went looking. They caught sight of a cleaning crew in their friend's house, a clear sign of struggle but no sign of the selkie. They never saw them again. They did catch the scent of the vampire who had been following them though.

"The hydra was far from their family's base and didn't want to lead this vampire to their remaining family, so they left the book with Thalia. She was looking after it until the hydra lost the man following them. The hydra didn't come to their last meeting and Thalia never saw them again. This book is hundreds of years' worth of paranormal history. The hydra started keeping track of those who went missing and couldn't be found. There's an entire section just for this. Gage, there are so many in here that are gone," he said brokenly.

He took a deep breath and held it, slowly letting it out. "Her letter goes on to say that our tribe's leader died, and she was too old to be able to lead them. He was younger than her, but she didn't mention how or why he died. Several younger members had already left, looking for better situations. The tribe was in chaos, no one certain who could take over. There was a lot of fighting for position. A man approached them, a vampire, who said that he knew of a place to go where they would be kept safe. Thalia didn't trust him, and she left a sketch of him. If we can find who he is or was, maybe that will help. Her last note said she stumbled upon proof that people were being taken. However, she was getting weaker and wasn't sure if she would be able to make it back to the other settlement to get the proof, but if she did, she would add it to this. I didn't see anything in here that would be concrete proof though. She wrote that she didn't want to wait in case the stranger came back, so she buried this package. She heard some of the tribe saying they were going to take the man up on his offer of a new home."

"Do you think that's what happened?" Gawain asked. They hadn't found any evidence that the settlement had been attacked or even a lot of bodies that would indicate there had been a major illness to kill them off.

"Maybe. If some had left already, then some left with the stranger, there wouldn't have been a lot of the tribe remaining. They would have died out or eventually need to leave too. It would be hard to survive with only a few members there. My guess is that after Thalia passed, any remaining members would have left. I can't see them leaving her on her own, especially since she was so old. She was the elder and the healer for the tribe and our laws and traditions demanded respect for her. That would be my best guess. I haven't come across any other unicorns since my last visit with Thalia," Doc said.

Gawain was digging through the materials, taking notes in his notebook. Merri was helping keep the desk organized. Gage walked over, looking at Doc for permission before touching anything on the table.

"Everything is there. There are some that aren't pleasant to read," he warned them.

As much as Marge didn't want to know, she needed to help her family. Picking up a few papers, she started reading. There were a few telegrams, a few newspaper articles about missing persons. The last paper in her hand was a letter. She felt sick to her stomach as she read.

My dearest sister,

I wish I could see you, but this letter will have to suffice. I cannot come home ever again. A man came to our village, asking about local myths and legends (just like the current flyers, Marge thought). *We didn't say anything, but he stayed a few days. I was in the garden, encouraging the plants to grow. I've managed to cause a few to change colors. He saw me. He was snooping around the corner and peeking through the fence. I locked all the doors, but I awoke to a man in my bedroom. I was ensnared in his gaze and could not move. It was terrifying. I must have fainted because the next thing I knew, I was chained in a room. A different man was in there with me. He was also chained. He was a shifter. Our abductor came in, saying he chose us for our gifts. We should be grateful because he would keep us safe. He wanted us to mate, to give him children that should be extraordinary. That was the word he used, extraordinary.*

The man with me was a gentleman, never making an untoward move. We spent days and weeks talking and became good friends. Our captor lost patience with us and began cutting our rations. Gerald would always make sure I ate, even if he gave up his own food. Finally, we were told that if we didn't mate, then there would be no more food. Gerald tried to give me all of his last meal. We hid it and ate it as long as possible. He was so weak, I finally convinced him to be physical with me. We were good friends, and I didn't want him to die. Even though I didn't love him like a mate, I still loved him as a friend. It wasn't bad, he made sure it was pleasant for me, but it still was something I wanted to save for my mate. I don't regret it though. We got another meal as soon as we were done. Gerald never initiated contact, but if we didn't have intercourse, we didn't eat. We tried to limit it to once a week, but we soon discovered that I was with child. Gerald didn't want our child to grow up there and be captive. We pretended that nothing had changed, but he helped me focus on my magic, having the weeds grow in our room, twine together to form ropes and I even managed a tiny ladder. It took a lot out of me, and Gerald gave me his food so I could keep my strength up. I think we managed to hide my condition because they never came into the room with us. We also didn't get the chance to really bathe, so I'm sure our…aroma covered the beginning scents of conception.

He lied to our captor and said that his kind of shifter needed the moonlight of the crescent moon every month or they weakened. Eventually they would die from it. It had been several moon cycles already. Gerald was very weak, but it had to do with the lack of food. Our captor agreed to let him out, and he requested I be allowed to come as well. It was an aphrodisiac to his shifter side to be under the moon, he told him. Our captor was, of course, ecstatic at that and agreed. We walked around the small enclosure. The walls were too high to climb, but there was no roof, so the potential for escape was there. Gerald had me face the wall, throwing my dress up over my backside, pretending to mate. I was actually encouraging the plants to grow, forming my ladder. It was sparse and not very sturdy, looking back at it, but in the moment, I was desperate for us to escape. Gerald shoved a biscuit in my dress pocket, the last of our food. He said I should climb first. If we got separated, to head to his family. They were hidden and didn't trust outsiders. I would be safe there. He had secretly been giving me directions for weeks. He gave me his bracelet to prove to them I was with him. I also had his scent all over me from living together.

We knew we were being watched and had to move quickly. As soon as the ladder was done, Gerald encouraged me to climb. We heard shouting and I have never climbed so fast in my life. I got to the top of the wall and looked down. Gerald shouted for me to take the ladder and go. I did not want to leave him; I swear to you. He rushed off, fighting to keep me safe and give me time. I still waited. I had pulled the ladder up to keep the guards from climbing, but I was going to throw it down for Gerald when he came close again. He never made it back. A guard stabbed him, and I watched him fall, his eyes on mine. He shouted for me to go and tripped the guard coming toward me. I lowered the ladder to the other side and ran.

I ran for days, stopping at small streams for water. The biscuit kept me going for a day, but food and water were sparse. I almost gave up hope, but finally reached his family. They were understandably upset and didn't want to believe me, but with some of the private stories Gerald told me, along with his scent and bracelet, they came to believe me. They have welcomed me, but I do not want to put anyone else in danger. I will not be disturbed here, and they are nice enough and will keep us safe. I wish you could know your niece or nephew. I will tell them about you. I will not risk anyone else, so this is my last letter to you.

I love you sister and wish you a lifetime of happiness,
Bella

Marge wiped her eyes, not wanting to drip tears onto the paper.

"What's wrong?" Duncan asked, wrapping his arms around her.

"This is horrible," she said. "They've ruined so many lives."

Duncan took the letter from her hand, swallowing hard as he read it. He silently passed it around the table.

"I hope she found some happiness," Shaye said quietly, also wiping tears from her eyes.

"This gives us something though," Marco said as he read the letter.

"What?"

"If this was Barry or his father, they have the ability to paralyze someone with their gaze. As much as folklore says vampires can ensnare their victims, it really isn't a very common gift. My guess would be his father, since Barry is using his power as a Convocation member to kidnap people. It would be much easier and draw less attention if he could simply paralyze and take someone at night. Also, that they have a compound somewhere. If the weeds and water were sparse, my guess would be somewhere desert-like, somewhere out west. They may have moved since this letter, but if we could find remnants of the building it might give us some clues. To move any group of captives would be an undertaking, so maybe they're still there," Marco explained.

Gage looked thoughtful, but he had an apologetic look on his face when he looked at Marge.

"Marge. Have you gone through that shipment yet?" Gage asked.

She shook her head. "No. I know it's silly. But I haven't wanted to go near it. The last time I did..." The last time she had been near it, she had been kidnapped.

"It's not silly, it's perfectly reasonable. And normally I would never tell you how to do your job, you know that. But I need you to go through those and see if you can find what Barry was looking for. I believe that whoever sent the box to you, did it to keep those things safe. In light of what Doc has, we have to try to get ahead of this," Gage said.

Marge nodded. "It's the first day of school tomorrow and we're going to be busy after school lets out. I can't just close the library; it's where a lot of kids go instead of going home to an empty house because their parents are working, or they meet a tutor or study group there."

"I can come help in the kids' area," Emma offered.

"I'll come in too, take over the main desk," Merri said. It was usually her off day, but this was more important and the things at the museum could wait. It was nearly perfect, and the last little bits could wait if they had to.

"I'll be there too," Duncan added. If there were any documents like the ones Doc had found, he wanted to be there. Either as physical or emotional support. Plus, he knew Emma still had anxiety attacks, although she had been getting better. To be in the library with the potential of a lot of strangers nearby was a big step for her. The kids' area should be a little less crowded, but he would still feel better about keeping an eye on all of them.

Marge took a deep breath and walked through the door, Duncan giving her a kiss.

'Call if you need me,' he said.

She nodded and shut the door behind her. She had a notebook to keep track of what she found in which documents, her phone fully charged, and she had her charger as well. She wasn't comfortable having the items out of the library, even with the town wards. There was only one box of things to go through. Granted it was a fairly large box, but that's what she told herself. Just one box. She had planned on using the desks to help her separate. One desk would be for items that were for the library but not dealing with this issue, one desk for items that might have to deal with this issue, and the other table for items that definitely were what she was looking for.

She'd ask Merri to double-check her sorting of the no and maybe piles later.

She took a bracing sip of her coffee and took the first item out of the box. She wore cotton gloves, since some of these looked really old. She skimmed the parchment, not finding anything sticking out and placed it on the first table. A lot of these top items were simply old paranormal documents, a few letters, some fairy tales, and history books. As she got closer to the middle of the box, she started running into a few maybes. There were a few vague references, but nothing concrete. Still, with dates on some of them or references to other events going on, they could at least get a better idea of the timeline. The book she had briefly glanced at when she had tried going through the box before her kidnapping had been toward the bottom. As she picked it up, a piece of paper fluttered down.

Bending down to grab it, she saw it was a newer piece of paper, not matching anything else in the box age-wise. *"Please keep this safe. Trust no one,"* she read. "Okay then." Although if the person who sent this had found out a Convocation member was corrupt, she guessed that the message would make sense.

Opening the book, she found a list of paranormals. This was double the one that Doc had received from Thalia. There were listings of extinct ones, what each species had for strengths and weaknesses. There was a section that speculated on other species. According to this book, Fate only allowed one of certain species to exist at a time to keep the balance. They were meant to help other paranormals and guide them. They could have mates and children, but the thought was that their children would be a different species or take after their other parent. The book cited a personal reference to a manticore they knew. He had a mate, a witch. Their children had been born mostly witches, although a couple had been lions. There was no telling what made them which species, the author wrote. The book mentioned the true immortality of some. Each section also had a last known area where the different species mainly lived. Lots of people moved, but it would give someone hunting them a place to start. The listing for jackalopes wasn't too far from where she knew some lived. There were a few sketches in here as well of some of the lesser-known species. This book would be dangerous if someone like Barry got a hold of it.

No wonder why Barry wanted this book so much. This was like a shopping list for him.

23

Marge brought the materials she had found and laid them on the table. Well, it was copies, the originals still safe at the library. This past week had been about digging deeper into the shifter registry, as she called it, and double-checking the other documents in the box. Merri had also gone through the papers, finding a few things that were cross-referenced in Doc's items. Merri and Gawain had been working on investigating and researching any information, families, or dates mentioned in the papers and books. They had formed a rough timeline.

Each of them had reached out to trusted friends to see if there were any rumors of hunter activity or paranormals going missing. She knew Emma's friend and farm caretaker, Douglas, was reaching out to the vast gnome network. Those guys really kept an ear out for the latest news and gossip. If there was something to be heard, they would know it or know where to seek it out. He was being cautious in his questioning at Emma's urging. Marge knew she was trying to keep her friends and their children safe. It may be a while before they heard anything back.

While they waited for any news to come in, there was

another family meeting tonight to go over what everyone had found. Tomorrow was the grand opening of the Paranormal History Museum. They wanted to grab this time to catch up with their discoveries before life got even busier. Plus, you never knew who might stop into the museum and it would be smart for them to have all the information possible when dealing with whoever visited.

"Merri and Gawain have been working on trying to confirm the link to Barry. We can finally say that this was definitely his family who started this whole problem. We found an old family portrait. Barry had it on his desk. You can see it on his Convocation profile page, which I'm amazed Gawain noticed. It's small and in the background, but it's an exact match to Thalia's sketch. If it's not his dad, it's a relative who looks exactly like him," Gage said. "Marco snuck into his office to verify it."

Gawain jumped in. "We found a few documents that were buried deep, but Marco also, uh, liberated some from Barry's office. Well, he took photos, the originals are still here. Some of them were recruitment letters to his cronies, which worked since the DDT was formed."

Marge snorted. She had forgotten that his friend Rob called them Douchebag, Douchecanoe, and Twatwaffle.

"He explains a bit of his reasoning behind his theory, heavy in vampire superiority, just like Vlad. I'm still uncertain whether Vlad was just a similar-minded occasional ally or if he was working for Barry. It seems unlikely that Barry would be working for him, and Vlad's ego was so huge, that I'm guessing they were just occasional allies.

"It seems like Barry's father started 'collecting' what he viewed as endangered species. He thought the world was too dangerous and some of them were too stupid to survive on their own. He liked having the only ones in existence. He did have a breeding program; he forced paranormals to be together, just like in the letter left for Doc. If they produced a child, he took the child to add to his collection if they had a rare power or shifted form. I'm not clear on what happened to the normal child or the couples. Barry has no written record of this that we've found so far. We found a few more letters similar to the one we all read, but none of them mention what happened afterward to the 'unsuccessful' pairings and offspring.

"When he had a child of his own, he was clearly already crazy, and he passed this on to Barry, whether by genetics or teachings. Barry would help collect people to add to his father's collection," Gawain said.

"I went over some of the notes and medical charts Marco found. The problem with arranged matings is that they are often less likely to produce children. It's already hard enough to procreate as a paranormal, but it seems that Fate gives fated mates a higher chance of getting pregnant than non-fated mates. They were losing their collection because they couldn't exactly pair siblings together to produce a child. They discovered that the really rare paranormals, the one-of-a-kinds, weren't made from parents exactly like them. They had similar traits, for example my parents were unicorns. Barry started the current breeding program, thinking that if he got enough pairs, that he would eventually get some results with powers or the species he wanted. I don't know if he still has a forced breeding program, there's no notes that we've found so far on that, but we do know about the paid program he has going on. His father started the collection as a way to keep them "safe," as delusional as that is. Barry kept it going as a way to collect power. His plan is to either find a way to make himself immortal and/or find a way to continue his family line as he doesn't have a mate or child. It seems like all of his efforts have failed to reproduce himself," Doc explained.

"May Fate hae made him sterile," Ian muttered.

"He has notes on several files that indicate he tried

drinking their blood, even performing surgery and removing what he calls minor things like a baby toe or appendix, something not life-threatening. He would consume it in the hopes of absorbing the power, but no luck," Doc said. "He seems to think that if he collects the kids, they'll see him as their dad and be willing to fight for him."

"Eww."

"What's his end goal though? Why pair with human hunters? They're killing paranormals, not just capturing. I mean, if he thinks vampires are superior, why would he let human hunters kill them? Statistically, some of those are going to be vampires; their detectors only show if someone is a paranormal, not what kind. Like the ones who tried to kill Ian. They assumed he was a demon," Shaye said.

"Maybe the ends justify the means, in his mind. He can request they bring him a specific person, no questions. He supplies the detectors. If a few paranormals are lost along the way, so be it. If they don't die, then maybe they are the kind he really wants, the truly immortal."

"It's not like they can easily share their immortality though. I can't imagine anyone willingly letting him join their family. Plus, not everyone knows how to even perform the ritual to do that."

"But if he were to somehow succeed in his breeding program and one was born and he raised it as his own, then that child might because they thought he was their father. They would want to help their father, right?" Berkley added quietly.

Crap.

Marge trudged up the stairs, sick to her stomach thinking of all the things they had found. Rolf had purchased several large magnetic white boards with stands that he placed around the library. They were using them to track some things. It was horrifying to see it all laid out.

Emma took Jimmy to the kitchen when he came home from school to make cookies. He was going to bring some in to share with Dave tomorrow. At least that was one good thing that had happened recently. Duncan scooped her up, carrying her the last flight of stairs and to their room.

"Let's snuggle," he suggested, plopping her on the bed, bending over to take her shoes off. She slid her shorts down, pulling her top and bra off. She climbed under the covers, turning to watch as Duncan undressed. It never failed to get her aroused, all those muscles and tats. She wanted to lick each swirl with her tongue. As he climbed into bed, leaning back against the headboard, she moved to kneel between his legs and leaned forward to do just that, licking her way down from his neck, his chest, down his thighs. His markings mostly ended on his thighs, although he had a small streak down the back of his calves. Strangely enough, his penis didn't have any markings. She ignored his hard shaft for the moment, working her way up the other leg and then to his chest where she bit his nipple. She wanted to feel something wonderful and forget about the horrible things they had learned for a little bit.

"I need you," he said, his hips thrusting in the air.

Marge took pity on her mate and deep throated his cock, swallowing around the hard length. Her hand reached down to cup his balls, her thumb gently stroking back and forth over the skin. Pulling back for air, she slowly twisted her tongue around his length, swirling around him, collecting the precum at the tip.

Keeping one hand gently stroking his shaft, she cupped a hand under her mouth slowly spitting into her hand, brushing the trail off with her thumb. Using both hands, she started to jack him off, knowing that this position would cause her breasts to bounce in front of him with each stroke.

Soon enough, he growled, grabbing her around the hips, pulling her in to suck at her breasts, her nipples hard. He gently bit each one before laving them with his tongue. Marge kept stroking the steel-hard shaft, reaching down with one hand to tease the testicles.

"Mouth, please," Duncan grunted, his legs tensing as he got closer to his release.

Grabbing a deep breath, Marge swallowed him whole, taking him so deep his balls rested against her chin. Her eyes began to tear as she held her breath, her head bobbing up and down, never letting him leave her throat. With a shout, Duncan came. She waited until he was done before she slowly drew back and off him.

Duncan moved fast, tossing her back on the bed, causing her to scream a little. He spread her legs, shoving his head in her groin. His tongue reached out, teasing her clit, circling it, rubbing over it before he traced down her seam to her opening. Sliding two fingers in, he began to shallowly thrust his fingers, but it wasn't enough to make her climax. With a wicked glint in his eyes, Duncan lowered his head to her mons, his thumbs spreading her lips apart, baring her for his perusal. He licked his lips, but his tongue looked a little forked, his dragon side peeking out. Filling her with two of his fingers again, he slowly slid his tongue inside her. The dual sensations were incredible, his tongue rubbing in different ways than his fingers. She tensed as she realized his tongue was reaching much deeper than it should be able to, looking down, she saw his pupils were slitted, as his dragon side came further out. Oh gods, he had shifted his tongue, that's why it was so much longer. It was dexterous, sliding out to curl around her clit, the forked ends teasing it as the rest of his tongue tightened around the nub. With one last lick to her clit, he slid his tongue back in her channel, the nimble appendage swirling against her walls, finding her G-spot, and pressing against it while his fingers thrust and gave her the feeling of being full. Her channel was filled with warmth as his tongue heated. She felt her orgasm build as he hummed, causing his tongue to vibrate. "Almost," she cried out. Duncan surged up, filling her with his dick. It only took a couple of thrusts before she was soaring, her orgasm ripping through her and the heat of his release filling her.

24

T he whole family was scattered throughout the museum and the backyard. They had put a sign on the roof asking any flying shifters to go to the private fenced-in area in the backyard to shift and then enter through the front door. Even with the wards, they were careful how many entry points were available to the public. Berkley and Ian were currently in the backyard/parking area. Jimmy was also with them. Rolf added a picnic table out there and Jimmy had brought some books and his video games. He had already seen the museum, having gone to the walk-through with the rest of them last night. Emma and Doc were stationed upstairs, to keep Emma from being overwhelmed if there were a lot of people. Upstairs was paranormal only, so there would be less visitors, and she had a key to the office if she needed a break. Rolf and Shaye were in the main exhibit area.

Marge had closed the library early today so she could be here. She had a feeling the museum was going to be a big help to the paranormal community. She was helping with tickets and the gift shop, Duncan working with her. Merri and Gawain were about to open the doors and Marge took a peek out the window. There was already a bit of a line, a mix of humans and paranormals. She saw Steve and Marshall in the line.

"It's time," Gawain shouted excitedly.

Merri unlocked the doors, opening them to their first guests. The museum would be run by donations and Rolf's backing, but they still were having people check in for tickets as a way to monitor how many and who was coming in. There was a guest book as well. Gage was debating whether or not to tap into the library system and have the ticket system let them know if it was a banned paranormal or human. They were still trying to figure out how it would work and if they even needed it with the town's wards. There were already spells in place to detect whether a person asking for information was a human, paranormal, or a mate.

She handed out greetings and tickets, Steve giving her a bashful smile as he took his. She took a quick breath, noticing he didn't smell like a human any longer, but more like a tortoise. Grinning at Marshall, she handed him his ticket. She watched out of the corner of her eye as Steve made a beeline to Shaye, stopping to talk to her and wrap her in a big hug. Aw.

She saw lots of familiar faces from the library. Dave, Jimmy's friend was there with his parents.

"He's in the backyard, if you get bored in here," she told him when she saw him looking around. She knew his parents would probably be more excited to read everything than he would be.

His mom nodded. "Go take a look at everything and then you can hang out with your friend. Is there anyone there with them?"

"Ian and Berkley are back there. I think they brought a deck of cards, cornhole, and there are some snacks and drinks out there as well," Marge replied. She was happy the boys were getting along so well. She thought they both had needed a friend.

Mary and Bill from the bakery came in, adding a couple boxes of cookies to the appetizer buffet. Mary handed her an insulated bag. "Place this under the counter. It's for all of you when you get home tonight. I know you won't get much of a chance to eat while you're working."

"You're amazing. Thank you," Duncan said, grabbing the bag. He loved desserts.

It was a steady stream all afternoon. They had already set up appointments for a few paranormals to come back when it was quieter to meet upstairs.

Marco came strolling in from the side of the store, so he must have appeared in the backyard. "Just wanted to say hi. It looks good in here. I can't stay. I found another camp like before. May have to find some new homes or safe houses if there's kids there, so I may not be back tonight. Gage knows where I'm at. Tell everyone else it looks great, and I'll come back soon."

"Be safe," Marge said.

Marco nodded, looking around quickly before disappearing. Marge was disturbed at the idea of more kids being manipulated and used by Barry. What kind of person had kids for money and then gave them up to a monster? Before she could work herself up too much, another wave of people came in the front door, distracting her. The rest of the time went quickly, visitors keeping them busy. Jimmy and Dave popped in for some of the mini burgers but took them outside to eat. She could hear their laughter as they played whatever game they had. Every so often she would hear the deeper tones of Ian and Berkley join in. He would be tired tonight; he had been out there all day.

A few minutes before closing, Gage came in looking exhausted. "Hey. This looks great. I haven't seen it since I helped with all the wards."

Rolf came over. "The food is pretty well decimated. Why don't you come back to the house for dinner? Mom put some soups in the slow cookers this morning and Tess made corn-bread muffins before we left."

"You don't mind?" Gage asked.

Shaye laid her hand on his arm. "Don't be silly. Come to dinner."

Marge watched as some of the tiredness left Gage, his shoulders relaxing. "Okay. I'll help clean up."

It didn't take long for them to finish. Duncan went upstairs to collect Jimmy, who had gone into the office with Emma once his friend had left.

Gage followed them in his car back to the house.

The soups smelled wonderful as they walked in. Rocke-feller greeting them with his bowl. Emma laughed but moved to get his dog food, adding some pieces of raw steak on top. "Thank you for being such a good boy while we were gone," she said, kissing the giant wolfdog between his eyes.

They were pretty quiet during dinner, all of them hungry. Happy, but hungry and tired from the busy day.

"Gage, you said something earlier when I invited you to dinner that I wanted to address. You are always more than welcome here. Marco too. Stop in, stay over, ask for help, come for meals, or just to hang out. You're part of our family. If you ever wanted to join officially—" Rolf started to offer, breaking off when Gage shook his head.

"I'd love to, but I can't. Part of being a Warden is not having a Clan or Tribe or Pack of your own. I guess they think it would cause favoritism or something."

"Well, you're still one of ours regardless. I can always reach out telepathically to you, if that's okay?" Rolf asked.

"That would be faster to let me know if something happened," Gage agreed. "Now, if Fate ever blesses me with a mate, my mate could technically join the Clan and I could piggy back the link that way as well.

"Thank you though. I never want to impose. But this means everything, and I do consider you all family now,"

Gage added softly. "I'll pass on the message to Marco too. It's just been the two of us for so long, it will take us a while to get used to being part of a family again. I'm a little stuck in my ways, as I'm sure Marge can tell you."

"It's true," Marge said, nodding emphatically.

Duncan could understand. He had been on his own for so long that it still took him aback that he had people he could call family. It was nice to feel wanted and if they needed help, they had a support system now. Like if he was caught up in a sculpture and Marge was at work, there were plenty of people for Jimmy to hang out with or pick him up from school. Even though he loved being here at the Clan estate, he was looking forward to moving into the library apartment too. He had never known people quite like these. Rolf didn't ask for anything in return, he was simply content to do what-ever it took to make his people feel happy. He had paid for the workshops and the additional enormous garage that housed their cars, Gawain's RV, and Ian's trailer. They had barely known him but welcomed him in and helped save his mate. They were an amazing group of people who genuinely cared for each other. He couldn't think of a better group to call family or to raise a child in.

"How about some dessert?" he asked, trying to lighten the mood. "Mary brought over a box just for us."

"I'll go get the coffee started," Shaye offered.

"I'll get the tea kettle," Emma said, joining Shaye in the kitchen. Marge followed them to help plate the desserts. The box was stuffed full of cookies, scones, mini cupcakes, and cheesecakes. She grabbed a large platter and made a dessert tray, bringing it out with a bunch of napkins. It only took a few minutes before the tea and coffee came out as well. Ian grabbed the remote and threw on a light-hearted comedy movie, helping everyone relax.

It was close to the end of the movie when Marco popped in. He sat on the floor by his brother. When Gage looked at him and opened his mouth, Marco shook his head. Gage simply put his hand on his shoulder and gently squeezed. Marge wasn't sure what happened, but Marco looked wiped out, stress lines near his eyes. She wanted to say something but wasn't sure what. She gave a small sigh of relief when she saw Shaye grab a cup of tea and a cookie, bringing them over to Marco. Once her hands were empty, Shaye laid a hand on Marco's shoulder, leaning down to talk to him quietly. Marge watched as she worked her magic, the stress lines lightening and his demeanor relaxing a little bit.

"I think it's time for bed, Jimmy," Duncan said. He had seen the interaction as well and figured Marco wouldn't want to talk about what happened in front of the boy. It was late anyway, and he had played outside for hours with his friend. "Head on up and brush your teeth. I'll be up in a minute to tuck you in."

Ian jumped up, bringing a bucket of ice back into the room. He grabbed some whiskey glasses and a bottle. "I hae a feeling we're going to need this," he said, pouring a shot into each glass.

Duncan grabbed his, adding some ice, before heading up to make sure Jimmy was in bed.

"Rock, go guard Jimmy," Emma said softly. If the dog was in the room with him, Jimmy was more likely to stay in bed and cuddle the dog than sneak back down to hear what they were talking about.

The wolfdog ran up the stairs after Duncan, who came down a few minutes later. Berkley cast a silencing dome over the room, just in case, and nodded to Marco.

"It was another breeding camp. It seems Barry's cleaning up after himself though. Everyone was dead. He didn't even try to hide it, the bodies were lying out, some of them drained, some of them torn apart. I don't know who he has working with him, because I don't see him doing all of it on his own. There were too many scents for me to filter out, which is saying something because I can normally figure it out pretty quickly. Maybe they used a spell of some sort, I don't know. There was evidence of children being there, but none of the bodies were kids. Either they escaped, but I couldn't trace any leaving the camp, or Barry took them," Marco said, his voice heavy.

"Do we have any idea how many of these camps there are?" Berkley asked.

Marco shook his head. "There hasn't been anything to indicate where they might be, at least not that I've found yet. I've been going through any notes or clues that I can find, and just happened upon an electric bill for this place. It was paying for several homes, which I thought was weird, and it was under his personal account, not the Convocation's bank."

"Can we trace them that way?" Sam asked.

"Maybe. The one I found Jimmy's parents at was under another name. His cronies at least know about the camps, since one of them was paying the bills on that one. I'm going to comb through their financials as much as I can to see if any more stick out. If we can get to them before he does, we can save the kids and maybe get a few witnesses to testify against him. Right now, it's a lot of circumstantial evidence. To really bring him down and brought to justice, we need to have something concrete. The TruthSpeakers will be able to force him to testify, but no one is going to want to take that step without proof of wrongdoing."

"What can we do to help?" Rolf asked.

"Not much for now. I don't want to draw his attention even more toward you guys. He failed with Marge and knows a dragon saved her, but I'm not positive he knows Duncan came from the town. I'm sure he researched the town before grabbing her and would have known there wasn't a dragon living here then, so he may have thought it was a random shifter passing by and not associate it with you. If he finds out you're looking into his business, he might get a lot more interested in you and the town. I know the town has its wards, but I also don't want to put them to the test. Some of the townspeople do leave for shopping or work, and I don't want them to in any way suffer for this. Keep your ears open if people come through, or like if Rick, Rob, or Daryl would reach out. Doc, if you and Gage can keep an eye on the forum for any problems? Gawain, I might need you for research later, if you and Merri would be willing to help."

"Of course," they agreed.

25

Duncan headed upstairs at the end of Marge's shift. The basement apartment was finally finished, and he had been moving furniture around with Rolf's and Ian's help. Berkley and Sam were working but were going to stop by when they were done to help with anything left over. Sam had sent lunch over as an apology for not being there. His manager had called in sick, and he had to go in on his day off. Duncan thought the apartment turned out wonderful. He had a few surprises for Jimmy in his room.

The biggest surprise had been Marge though. She had embraced moving everything around and she had gifted him a few things for his hoard. He wasn't as bad as other dragons about amassing a huge hoard, but he did have a small one. They were just things he liked; he wasn't picky about only collecting certain things like some dragons were. Marge had framed a picture of their whole family from the day they had joined the Clan and Tribe. The frame had some rocks from the woods where he found her, Jimmy's stubby pencil, and little pieces that represented everyone. It was amazing. He was sure it didn't look like much to anyone else, but to him it represented his family. His dragon had claimed the caves as his own and they had worked at setting up additional wards to keep everyone but family out. Most of his collection would be in a smaller space in the cave, but the photo would stay in the apartment.

"We've got a problem," Rolf said, following him up the stairs. He was looking down at his phone, eyebrows drawn tight.

"What?" He thought the basement was finished. They had the electric and plumbing checked out and it had all cleared. The furniture was in place. He stocked the fridge. Heck, even the beds were made.

"There's a Convocation member outside the ward asking to meet with us," Rolf said. "They're demanding to see Jimmy. How the hell did they even know who he was or that he's here? Barry kept him hidden while he had him."

"Let me call Gage before we head out to the front desk," Berkley said, walking into the break room. "I think we're going to want him and Marco to be aware of this."

He put his phone on speaker, the three of them listening to it ring for several seconds before he picked up.

"Hey. I was just going to call you. Are you guys sensing something outside of town?"

"I just got a message on my phone from someone claiming they're from the Convocation and want to meet with us. They're outside the wards and want us to come there. They want to see Jimmy."

"FUCK!" Gage shouted. "Okay. Let me call Marco. Get some of the Clan together as a show of support, or strength. Whichever way they take it. Duncan, can you grab Jimmy from school, it's about lunchtime so he won't miss too much? Rolf, make sure Doc stays back. I don't want him to be visible to whoever is here. I don't know if we can trust them yet. We'll just say he had patients and couldn't get free, if they ask.

"I don't want to piss them off, on the chance that they

would be on our side, but I don't want to show our hand if they're with Barry either."

"I'm thinking me, Sam, and Berkley should be there as founding members in this town. Shaye, in case there are problems and as my mate. Marge and Duncan as Jimmy's parents. Gawain since he's done a lot of research and can explain what's been happening with history and facts to back it up. His name is well known and should lend credence," Rolf said. He wanted to keep Doc away from everyone. His mom wouldn't do well with the stress and the new people, so she could help Doc at the clinic.

"I think Tess should be there," Sam said. "As much as I don't want her near any potential danger, she and Berkley together make a great magical team, and the ward will keep us safe. If they try messing with it, they'll be able to counteract it."

"Agreed," Gage said. "We're also not going to mention anything about Shaye's abilities. They're rare enough that they would be intriguing if they're with Barry. You guys met when she came here for a job, and she decided to turn to be stronger against Vlad. Pretty much the truth, just missing a few pieces. Berkley, keep in contact with Ian. He's the fastest of us and can come grab Jimmy if we need to get him away. Let's have Merri stay at the library, Ian at the Winged Potter, Emma and Doc at the clinic. It shouldn't draw too much attention from the townspeople if some of us are still in our normal spots."

Rolf nodded, sending out a telepathic call to the Clan. He briefly explained what was going on and promised to leave the link open so that they could all be kept in the loop. Duncan left to get Jimmy while they waited for the rest of the family to arrive. Rolf sent a response back to the Convocation member, stating they would be there in a few minutes.

Marge came over, both angry and worried. She was silently fuming, not wanting to spread even more stress among her family. With all the bullshit Barry had been involved in, they chose to harass them? Seriously? They were just trying to live their lives, not causing any problems. Heck, Rolf, Sam, and Berkley had lived in this town for about a hundred years and never had any problems until the Vlad incident last year. And that had been contained, the towns-people never even knew it happened. Plus, getting rid of Vlad was like a gift to the Convocation; he had been a huge problem for everyone. And now they may be here trying to take her son away. Over her dead body.

Shaye and Tess came in, still in their scrubs from work. Tess went to talk to Sam, who wrapped her in his arms, holding her tight. Shaye stopped at Rolf, giving him a gentle kiss, murmuring to him softly. Marge watched the door intently, waiting for her mate and son. She startled when she felt an arm wrap around her waist, Shaye's head resting on her shoulder as she stood next to her.

Marge let out a deep breath, letting Shaye's calming vibes spread through her. She hadn't realized she had clenched her muscles so tight. "Thank you," she said, the anger fading and letting her more logical side come out. The cat side of her had been hissing mad at the thought of a threat to her kit. "You should probably give everyone a hug," she said with a half laugh. "I think we're all kind of worked up."

"It's not a bad idea," Shaye agreed. "I think if we're all calm, it will throw them off. I think by showing up unan-nounced they wanted to shock us. If we're calm and unthreat-ened, it may surprise them enough that they let something slip. If nothing else, it will maybe show we don't have anything to hide."

Duncan arrived with Jimmy, Gawain coming in behind them.

Gage explained the situation again, stressing not to say anything about Doc or Shaye's powers. He also asked Rolf to keep a telepathic link open with him so if needed, Gage could send a message to everyone. Marco popped in, distrust and anger on his face.

"Let's go see what bullshit this is going to be," Marco said.

"Hold on," Shaye said. "Marge recommended this. Everyone, hold hands," she instructed. Marco and Gage looked at her questioningly, but they joined in with everyone else. Marge could feel the tension in the room sharply drop as Shaye used her gifts. It was pretty amazing she had a healing and an empath gift that allowed her to sense their emotions and to help calm them down. Marge knew they would all think a lot clearer if they were calm and not overwhelmed with worry, fear, or anger.

As a group, they climbed into Gage's marked police SUV and Rolf's SUV and headed toward the edge of town. Marge noticed that Shaye had pulled her pendant out so that they would all be able to see if it glowed. The alert to danger would be helpful today.

Pulling up to the edge of the town's boundaries, they noticed another vehicle on the other side. There were two people standing by the car.

'Gage says the one on the left is a TruthSpeaker. We're going to have to be very careful in what we say. It needs to be the truth, but try to leave enough out to protect ourselves,' Rolf cautioned. *'The Convocation member isn't one known to be with Barry, but neither Gage nor Marco knows where she stands. She's not one of the ones they know and trust.'*

Jimmy grabbed her hand, leaning hard into her side. The poor kid had finally gotten a glimpse of a normal life and had come out of his shell, relaxing around all of them. He had a home where he was loved, and she knew everyone here would do their best to protect that.

'Everyone ready? Let's get this over with,' Rolf said, turning off the car.

"Good afternoon," Rolf said, walking closer to the other two. He made sure to stay on their side of the ward. The rest of them stood in a half-circle behind him, Gage on one side, Marco on the other. "What is this about? I'm happy to speak with you, but I would request that it be somewhat quick. We all have jobs or school to get back to," he said firmly.

Marge had never heard this tone of voice from Rolf before. It was authoritative and stern, but not unfriendly. It certainly made him sound like the Clan leader he was.

The Convocation member cleared her throat. "Yes, well thank you for meeting with us. We have some questions about the happenings in your Clan lately."

"Have we missed some paperwork of some kind? I thought we had filed all the needed documents," Rolf stated. Marge almost grinned at the unassuming opening lines. It would certainly cause them to have to state their intentions clearly. It was a good move.

"No, the Clan paperwork was all in order. It has to do with something else."

Rolf simply waited; his head tilted questioningly. When it became clear he wasn't going to speak, the Convocation member finally spoke up.

"We have questions regarding your involvement with Barry and how you came to get this boy adopted into your group. We also have questions for Marco, that we'll deal with at a later time," she said. Marge couldn't tell if that was a threat or not, but she was sure between Rolf and Gage, they would handle it.

"We're not involved with a Barry. I'm assuming you mean Convocation member Barry," Rolf said.

"Yes." She looked at the TruthSpeaker standing next to her, who replied with a small gesture. "Tell us more about Barry," she demanded.

Gage stepped forward. "I believe he already stated he wasn't involved with Barry, ma'am. May I ask why you're questioning members of my jurisdiction? I can assure you they have done nothing wrong."

"It's come to our attention that there have been several incidents around this town and the Nightwood Clan members. It's very concerning."

"So concerning that none of you have offered to help?" Marco said, a bit of a bite to his voice.

"I wouldn't say much, Marco. I think you stink of this," the woman said.

Rolf squared his shoulders, anger filling his face. "I don't know who you are. We haven't seen any ID, and you brought a TruthSpeaker with you, signaling your intentions. These Wardens have done nothing but protect paranormals and the humans that live in this town. I suggest that you clearly state your question and identify yourself, or leave. You didn't even have the common courtesy to come into our town and introduce yourself to our Sheriff and local Warden."

"Fine. We can play it that way," the woman said angrily, her cheeks flushing. Turning to the man next to her, she said, "Get what I need."

26

Marge pulled Jimmy to stand between her and Duncan. This wasn't going to end well. No one was able to hide from a TruthSpeaker, that's one of the reasons why Barry had taken Jimmy.

"Where is the rest of your Clan?" the man asked, a small tendril of power reaching out. The ward let it through, not sensing a danger. Marge wondered if they could fix that later, but they may also need Jimmy's powers one day and didn't want them limited.

"At work, like I already told you. If all of us disappeared, it would look suspicious to the town," Rolf said honestly.

"What kind of people are in your Clan and what are their powers?"

"We have all kinds of paranormals in my Clan. We're a family. We have witches, shifters, vampires. You don't need to know their powers, it's none of your business," Rolf said, clenching his teeth with the effort not to blurt out everyone's secrets. It really was none of the Convocation's business; you didn't have to register your powers at all. In fact, it was considered a highly personal matter.

"You stand out. We need to know," the man said,

throwing a little more power behind it. Because Rolf had the Clan link open, they could feel the TruthSpeaker poking at Rolf's mental shields, trying to find a weak spot. If he threw his full power behind it, the shields would shatter. Once a TruthSpeaker went full force with their powers, there was no keeping secrets or blocking them from reading you; they gained full access to your mind. Marge felt Shaye stir along the Clan link, wrapping herself around Rolf's mind. Marge knew he had a shielding ability but wasn't sure how long he could maintain it.

"You don't. That's never something the Convocation has demanded before. You're out of line," Marco said, standing in front of Rolf to block the TruthSpeaker's view.

"We can start with you then. You've been traveling a lot, leaving your stink places it doesn't belong. We know you've been to Maine recently. What were you doing there?" the man demanded, everyone feeling the force of his power as he threw it at Marco.

"I was investigating," Marco said. "We had discovered some disturbing things, signs that that someone was doing something illegal, and I was following a lead. I found the breeding camps. Everyone was already dead by the time I arrived at the last one. At the first camp I arrested some, relocated others," he answered. "I tried to find out who was behind them, but didn't find anything concrete, just a few bills that linked back to bank accounts."

"Why and who did you kill?" the man demanded, his full power flowing now.

Marco's body strained as he tried not to answer.

Jimmy tugged her hand, pulling her up to stand by Marco. Marge let him pull her closer, but only because Shaye's pendant wasn't glowing to alert to danger yet. She could see the fine lines of stress on Marco's forehead ease as Jimmy stood next to him.

"I didn't kill anyone," Marco lied smoothly.

What the hell? How was he able to do that? Marge was shocked. They all knew that Marco had killed Jimmy's parents to keep him safe.

"Everyone here saved me," Jimmy said quietly. "Barry took me from my parents and school and kept me for two years. They're dead. Barry stole Marge and hurt her very badly. When they saved Marge, they saved me too. Marge and Duncan adopted me. All the paperwork has been filed. Barry is a lying, horrible person who hurt me and a bunch of other people. He paid people to have kids, he kidnapped others. You should be stopping him instead of being mean to my family." Jimmy stepped forward to have his toe touch the ward. He didn't cross it, just touched where it was. Suddenly, the other TruthSpeaker's power seemed cut off. She could still sense it, but it wasn't overwhelming like before.

"What about the rest of you?" he questioned, his power fully immersed in his voice demanding answers and he let it spread out over all of them. "What do you know about Barry and these camps?" Marge could feel it was stronger, trying to make them answer, but it was like a light breeze blowing over her; she had no compulsion to answer.

'Gage and I got this one,' Rolf told them.

"Just like Marco told you, and I'm sure Gage has submitted a report. Our town's librarian, who also happens to be the Guardian, was kidnapped. Her mate was visiting town and caught her scent. He helped us search for her. When we found her, she was extremely injured and malnourished. It's also where we found the boy. They both pointed to Barry as their kidnapper. Marco began the hunt for his parents, which led to him being found to be an orphan. Marge and the boy had bonded during their captivity, and he was comfortable with them. There were no other relatives and they wanted to adopt him. The town is a safe place for paranormals and a good place for him to grow up," Rolf said.

"How do you know she didn't make it up?"

Duncan growled at that question, but Marge put her hand on his arm, holding him back. Why in the world would she make it up? She wasn't sure what their game plan was here. What were they really looking for?

"She was near death. She never heard his name; the others didn't address him by name. Based on her description, it sounded a lot like Barry. I showed her pictures of the Convocation members for the last two hundred years. And before you say something, all names were removed. I even added photos of random people I found on the internet. There were enough people in the images I showed her that she didn't know I was looking at a Convocation member, but she picked him out without any hesitation. She also identified his assistant as one of the ones who had kidnapped and abused her. The boy had been held captive by Barry and hidden away for two years. He knew who he was," Gage responded.

"Why do you have a ward around your town?"

"This is meant to be a safe place for humans and paranormals. After Vlad and the kidnapping, we made sure it would stay safe," Gage said, crossing his arms over his chest. "There are also signs of hunter activity, which you would know if you read my reports. The ward keeps those with ill-intensions out, which makes me wonder why you're still on that side of it. Worried what it might do?"

"We only sensed there was a ward, not what kind. We also didn't want to be at the mercy of those who meant harm," the Convocation member stated.

"You're keeping things from us," the TruthSpeaker said.

"We've answered your questions. You used your power to force us to talk," Rolf pointed out. He was relieved that they hadn't asked more questions and was wondering how the power behind the TruthSpeaker seemed to have diminished.

"Barry isn't the only one involved. There are two others we know of. Quite frankly, we don't trust you. You came here, demanding to see us, don't have the balls to cross the ward, and then you use your gifts to force the truth from us without giving us much of a chance to do so willingly. We answered your questions. We're not going to give you more than we have to. If you're aligned with Barry, no good will come of us giving you more, and if you're not with him, you certainly aren't one we can trust," Marco spoke up. "When we have a concrete case, we'll make sure it goes to those who can be trusted."

"So, you're not anti-Convocation?" the TruthSpeaker demanded.

"No. We both work for the Convocation and the idea that the Convocation is there to protect its people. If someone is abusing that power, then they need to be dealt with, no matter their species or title," Gage said.

"We're on the same side here," the woman protested.

"Maybe. We'll see. Until we know for sure, we're not going to give you anything that could tip our hand. Our first goal is to protect paranormals under our watch. Second is to protect this town. This town has been good to us, and in return we'll continue to protect them. The people here are welcoming and will protect their own. Instead of harassing good paranormals, maybe try fixing the problem of those who are abusing their power. Find a way to stop them," Marco demanded.

"I'll look into it," she replied.

Marge wasn't going to hold her breath though. They still hadn't crossed the ward's border, nor had she volunteered her name. Maybe she thought she didn't need to because Gage and Marco were Wardens and knew who the Convocation members were, but it was still extremely rude.

"There's been whispers of his questionable actions for years, but it was always voted down to look into it. There were a handful of protestors, those who wanted him investigated, but there were just as many who voted not to. They were louder and had a few more numbers in the beginning, and the ones who didn't take sides usually didn't want any conflict," the woman continued.

"Like you," Rolf guessed.

She nodded. "I heard the stories. Even heard a few things from Barry himself that made me wonder. But I never did anything."

"Then part of this is on you," Marco said angrily.

"I'll be in touch if I find anything," she said, turning to get in her car. Her companion followed.

"Let's talk about this tonight. I don't want it to seem like anything is wrong; head back to work, and we'll talk at dinner," Rolf suggested. "Marco, Gage, that includes you," he said with a smile.

They piled back in the cars, heading into town. Marge was replaying the whole thing over and over in her mind. She honestly had no idea what the woman wanted. What she really wanted to know was how Jimmy had stopped the other TruthSpeaker from using their powers on them. It was the only thing she could think of that explained what happened.

"Do you want me to call you out for the rest of the day? You can hang out in the library or downstairs if you want," Marge offered as they got out of the car at the library.

Jimmy shook his head. "I want to go to school."

"Okay. No matter what, we all love you and this is your home," Duncan replied when Marge was about to protest. He figured the boy had gotten into a routine and he had read that having a routine made kids more comfortable.

A server from the Black Wolf Brewery ran over, holding a take-out bag.

"Thanks," Sam said, taking the bag from her. He walked over to them. "Here, Jimmy. I know we pulled you away from lunch and you probably didn't get a chance to eat. It's a burger and some fries, with a cookie for dessert. I figured you could eat it before you went back."

"Thanks, Sam," he said, giving him a hug. Looking in the

bag, he finally smiled and pulled out the chocolate chip cookie, eating it first.

"Thank you, Sam," Marge said.

"Anytime," Sam replied. "I'm heading back to work, but call if you need anything," he offered.

Marge and Duncan waited until Jimmy finished his food before walking him back. Gage joined them on the walk.

"I'm just going to pop into the principal's office and reinforce that only the family have the right to take him out of school," Duncan said as they got closer.

"I'll go with you," Gage said. They hadn't told much to the school, but he thought it was time to let them know Jimmy had been kidnapped from his last school by people pretending to be police officers. It would be good to talk to all the staff and let them know only their family had the rights to pick him up or take him out of school, no matter the reason. If someone tried the police trick again, it helped that he was the Sheriff in town. He would let them know he would be the only one to collect Jimmy. In case they changed their MO, he would also heavily imply that Marco worked for the government and was their point of contact if an official matter came up and they couldn't get ahold of him. He would tell them that all inquiries about the boy or the family should go to one of them. The wards should prevent any of that, but it never hurt to be prepared.

Marge locked up the library front doors, walking back to collect Duncan and Jimmy from the break room. Duncan had been helping him with his homework.

"Ready to go eat dinner? Emma said she was making a special dessert for tonight," Marge said, as Jimmy packed up his backpack.

"Sure," he answered. He still seemed a little subdued and withdrawn from this afternoon.

The meal was amazing as always, lots of comfort foods like bread and stew, some cheesy casseroles. They waited until after Jimmy had scarfed down his brownie and vanilla ice cream to bring up the events of the day.

Gage cleared his throat. "Jimmy, can you pay very close attention to me for one minute?"

He nodded, looking directly at Gage.

"No one can take you away. This is your home. Marco and I used spells to make sure that the documents cannot be altered in any way. The wards will keep anyone who wants or tries to take you away, out. Any one of us would fight to keep you here, understand?"

Jimmy nodded, a small, relieved smile on his face.

"Now we have to talk about the other thing," Marco joined in. "How did you stop the other TruthSpeaker from using his powers on us? It was working with Rolf and then when they got to the last question with me, you stopped them somehow."

Jimmy squirmed in his seat, anxious.

Marge leaned over. "Remember. We all love you, no matter what," she whispered to him.

"I didn't like it when he was forcing Rolf to answer, even though Rolf was doing a good job; I could tell he was shielding, and Shaye was helping. I've already guessed what Marco did to help me stay here and I didn't want him to get into trouble for it. Or any of you, since I think you know more than you told them. I started feeling tingly, all over, like when you put your hand on one of those electric balls that make your hair stand up? We had one in class; it was really cool. I let it kind of build up and flow around me and then I noticed I didn't feel his power as much. So, I thought if I stood next to Marco, I could let it flow over him too and maybe he wouldn't have to answer. When that worked, I wondered how I could get it to work for everyone, and thought if I touched the ward, and let it flow through the ward, then everyone would be protected," Jimmy said quietly, looking down at his hands, shredding the napkin.

"That was very smart of you," Gage praised. "Thank you for looking out for everyone."

"You don't think I'm weird? Is it normal? I've never heard of it before."

"I don't think it's very common," Marco said slowly. "I've never heard of it either, although I don't think anyone would advertise that they could sidestep the one thing the Convocation relies on to make people tell the truth."

"And if you're a little weird, so what?" Shaye interjected with a smile. "Embrace your weird. We all love you no matter what. Each one of us has something that someone else would consider strange. My own parents thought I was abnormal, even before I became a vampire. Rolf's father tried to kill him."

"Many people still dinnae accept that two men can have a loving relationship. And I hae to eat a lot more often than other people because of my metabolism," Ian added.

"I turn into a flying unicorn and I'm the only one," Doc pointed out.

"I have anxiety and sometimes can't leave the house," Emma said softly. Marge was grateful that those incidents were getting farther and farther apart. Emma had been blossoming and it was beautiful to see.

"I forget to eat when I'm working. Like for days if someone doesn't stop me," Gawain pointed out.

"Marco and I hide that we're brothers. He's a gargoyle and I'm a griffin, also the only one of my kind. We all have different gifts, but that's what makes us such a great family," Gage said, including himself as part of the family for the first time. Today had made him see that he really did think of them as family, not just friends. The fear he felt when he saw the Convocation member and the TruthSpeaker had been intense. He wasn't used to feeling fear. "We all are different, but we all accept each other that way. We make each other stronger. Like you did today. You lent your gift to help support and protect your family," he pointed out.

"Okay," Jimmy said, a huge smile on his face. He slipped a piece of beef to Rockefeller when he laid his head in his lap. The smile got even bigger when Emma sneaked him an extra slice of brownie.

They all gathered in the living room after dinner, no one seeming to want to separate quite yet. Jimmy eventually fell asleep, and Duncan carried him up to his room.

'Do you want to just stay here tonight? He's already sleeping, and I think everyone needs to feel close after today,' Duncan suggested.

'I do. There's no good reason to drag him back to the library. He has a change of clothes here and his school stuff already. We'll just leave a few minutes earlier in the morning,' Marge said. When they had been moving their stuff over to the apartment, Shaye told her that they were going to keep their rooms available for them and to keep a couple changes of clothes at the house. That way if they stayed late or Jimmy had a sleepover so they could have a date night, it would be easier on them. Marge was grateful for the foresight now.

Duncan grabbed a cup of coffee before coming to sit next to her on the couch. She leaned against him, her head resting on his chest, tucked under his chin. He moved his coffee to his left hand, using his right one to gently run his fingers through her hair. She had never really had anyone play with her hair before, but she found when he did it, it was very relaxing.

It took a few minutes, but Sam finally spoke up.

"What are we going to do about the visit today? Is it something we need to be worried about?"

"I didn't like the 'you stand out' comment," Berkley said quietly.

"I agree," Marco said. "I'm not really sure how you stand out either; you guys are quiet unless you're being attacked. I didn't even know most of you were here until Gage called me in. Maybe it's that your Clan isn't only vampires, you have a mix of all different types of paranormals."

"She really shouldn't have tried to find out what your animals and powers are. That's always been considered extremely personal. It's not an official rule anywhere but it is common practice not to ask, much less force, someone to tell you," Gage said. "Quite frankly, the line of questioning was bordering on abuse of power. They didn't have a good cause to question you, and they certainly didn't have a lie detector that would legally enable them to use their TruthSpeak powers. They skipped several steps. I don't know if she's with Barry and trying to get information or if she's freaked out and trying to hurry up to take action. Either way, she was out of line.

"We're going to contact the Convocation members we trust and see if they've heard anything, including anything about her. They're normally good about reaching out, which makes me think this wasn't an official visit even though she was using her position to force the meeting. But this way they'll know to keep their ears open. Gawain, can you reach out to Rob and see if he's heard anything new and if he can reach out to his contact as well? Since we still don't know if his friend is a Convocation member or someone who works there, it's better to cover all our bases. I don't trust her; even if she's not with Barry, she still sat by while hearing things he had done," Gage said.

"So, we just wait?"

"Yup."

EPILOGUE

"There's a warrant out for Barry's arrest! We already got the other two, but he seems to have disappeared. It's going to be hard for him to hide with his face plastered everywhere," Gage yelled out, rushing around the house into the backyard.

"Oh, that's good news!" Tess said, relief in her voice. They had all been worried that the Convocation wouldn't believe the evidence that Marco and Gage had submitted. It was the first time a Convocation member had been investigated. There had been the incident with a TruthSpeaker who worked for the Convocation many years ago, but they weren't technically a Convocation member, more of an employee.

They had also been worried that Marco would get in trouble from being scented at two of the breeding camps. Evidence turned up pointing to other locations and someone else had gone to investigate them. Most of the Convocation had believed Marco's reports, but a few had raised a stink wanting someone else to take over to make sure the next scene wasn't "tainted." When they arrived at the new locations, there had been no trace of Marco, solidifying their claims that he had been at the other two investigating.

The other camps had been in a similar state as the last one Marco had found; ransacked, children missing, and adults killed. There could have been adults missing as well, but without an inventory list, it was hard to tell. They still hadn't been able to find the main location of Barry's family's estate though, the place they thought the paranormals were being kept. It was odd that no one knew where he lived, not even his two cronies had any idea. Based on the letter they had found previously, they were still thinking it was out west.

What Gage hadn't told them until later was that he had used his magic to put a tracker on the Convocation member who came to visit. His magic let him leave a small undetectable piece of itself on someone, allowing him to track them. Just being near him left a small trace for a few minutes, but he could consciously leave a larger piece and track the other person. Marco was able to follow it and had been routinely checking in on the woman, making sure she wasn't aligned with or meeting with Barry. So far nothing she did seemed out of the ordinary. Maybe she had just been self-involved before and finally realized Barry needed to be stopped, who knows.

Ian and Berkley ran inside to get the meat and potatoes for the grill. Sam handed Gage a beer.

"Here, try this one for me," Sam said. "It's my Fall brew, but I haven't named it yet. You guys are my guinea pigs."

Gage snorted but took a sip. "Oh! That's good. It's got apples and cinnamon. Cloves, maybe?"

"Good taste buds," Sam complimented.

Marge smiled as she watched Gage walk over to the new hammock pavilion. Rolf had added another one this summer and it was getting a lot of use. He had added a few hammock chairs to this one, all outdoor ones that could withstand paranormals. Most of the guys were not small; they were tall and muscular, Gage being the tallest of them at six foot seven inches. Sam had claimed a double hammock, Tess in there with him reading a book. Once the potatoes and burgers were on the grill, Ian and Berkley each grabbed a hammock as well. Emma and Doc were snuggled up on a couch, Shaye lying with her head in Rolf's lap, reading on her phone. Duncan and Jimmy were playing catch in the yard. They had invited Marco as well, but he hadn't arrived yet. She knew Merri was upstairs with Gawain; he had discovered a few documents in a human history museum that he thought might be paranormal in nature and connected to the whole Barry debacle.

It was such a relaxing evening that it was a shock when Shaye's phone rang. They had all just sat down to eat. She looked down at it, frowning.

"That's Elliot. I wonder what he wants. I better take this," she said, getting up from the table.

"Hello," she said, walking away from the group so she could hear better.

It only took a few minutes before she was back again.

"Everything okay?" Rolf asked.

"Yeah," Shaye said slowly, confusion in her tone. "He's coming for a visit."

"Do you not want him to come?" Marge asked. She hadn't heard of an Elliot before and was curious. Shaye took his call, which meant she cared about him, but she wasn't jumping up and down for joy that he was coming to visit. If the guy was bad news, the town wards wouldn't let him in.

"No, I do. I haven't seen him in a while. He's an amazing baker; that's where I got the recipe for the cheesecake at Christmas. He never really leaves his family though. They all live in the same town, actually I think maybe it's in the same neighborhood, kind of like Tess's family. I met him when I had a work assignment there and we've kept in touch, but he's never wanted to leave home before. I'm just worried that something is wrong and he's not telling me," she admitted.

Marge looked at Duncan. While it wasn't unusual for families to all stay in the same town, they didn't normally live all in the same neighborhood unless they were paranormals grouping together. It was unusual that it was such a big deal for Elliot to leave. There had to be a story there, even if Shaye didn't know it.

"He'll tell you when he sees you," Tess suggested. "From the few times I've met him, he seems like a nice guy."

"He is," Shaye said. "Oh, and he's human, so I don't know what we need to do when he comes. Do we keep it all a secret or do we tell him?"

"Is he staying here?"

"No, he already has a room booked in town. I guess if he's not staying here, he won't see Doc's medical room and all the blood bags," Shaye replied. "I think you guys will like him though. I'll have to have him meet Mary and Bill and they can talk about baking. He's always wanted to own his own bakery, but he mostly sells out of his home and does a lot of mail orders."

"He does have some amazing food," Tess agreed.

NOTE FROM THE AUTHOR

Thank you for reading *Hoarded Secrets*! If you enjoyed the story, please consider leaving a review. Reviews, no matter how short, are invaluable to independent authors.

What happens with the hunters? Will they be able to stop Barry? Keep reading for a sneak peek into *Warded Bond*, book seven of the Nightwood Clan series.

If you keep flipping through after the Sneak Peek, you'll find the list of characters mentioned in the books. You'll also find room diagrams of Marge's apartment and the Paranormal History Museum.

G age knew he was scowling at his phone, but he couldn't make himself stop. Marco was due hours ago, but he wasn't here, and he wasn't responding to his phone calls. It was frankly starting to worry him. Tonight was the first time that Marco would be attending an Inebriated Inconsistencies night with the Clan, and he had been super excited to come. He had made sure it was in his calendar so he wouldn't miss it.

Gage tried reaching out over their telepathic link but was met with a blank space. He'd never run into anything like it before and it was freaking him out.

Elliot leaned into him. "Still can't reach him?" he asked quietly.

Gage shook his head.

"You should see if Rolf can help, somehow. He has telepathy as his gift, so maybe he can help boost you or something," he suggested.

"It wouldn't hurt to ask." Gage shrugged, getting up to find Rolf. He had been in the kitchen last time he saw him.

Turning the corner, Gage almost ran into him. "Hey, sorry about that. I was looking for you. I can't get ahold of Marco and at this point his phone goes straight to voicemail. Which has happened before, especially if he's working a case and doesn't want it to be heard. He normally finds time to check in though. The weirdest part, the part that is worrying me, is that I can't reach him over our link. I've never run into this before and wanted to see if you could try to boost me or see what you thought."

"Yeah, of course. I've linked with him before, so that should help. I'm going to link with you first, then you link with him, and we'll see what we get."

Gage felt and heard Rolf along the telepathic link and then he reached out to find his brother. Once again, he ran into blankness. There was no connection on the other side, or rather it was like it was blocked. He felt Rolf sending his own power through him, bolstering his signal as it were, but nothing changed. Rolf changed his tactic, feeling his way around the link, searching for something.

"I've got nothing," Rolf finally admitted. "I haven't run into this before. I can tell you he's alive; it feels vastly different than when I tried to connect to a deceased person. I'm…" Rolf trailed off, clearly thinking something.

"What?" Gage demanded.

"I'm not positive, this is just a thought that entered my head and I have no real basis for it, so take it with a grain of salt. Do you remember when Marge was taken? We couldn't scent her or track her because she had a Tamer spell on her. What if he has something similar? I didn't try to connect telepathically with Marge at the time, so I can't be sure this is right."

Gage listened, horror spreading through him at the thought. "I have a pair at the office for extreme cases. I hate using them because it cuts a shifter off from their animal which is horrible. Let me go get them, I'll put them on, and you can see if it feels the same."

Minutes later, he had the cuffs in hand and headed back to

the house. He gave his mate a quick warning that they would lose connection for a minute and handed Rolf the key. Slapping the cuffs on himself, Gage braced as his connection to his griffin waned. He could still feel him, but it was much fainter than normal.

Rolf stared at him, head tilted. "It's crazy. You're standing right there, I can touch you, but you suddenly stopped registering to my senses. It's like a blank wall trying to reach you as well. If Marco isn't in something with a Tamer spell, he's in something very similar because it feels alike," he said, sympathy in his face.

"Crap."

NIGHTWOOD CLAN

LOCATION

The series is mainly set in Rockfort, Tennessee, a fictional town next to the Great Smoky Mountains National Park.

CHARACTERS

Rolf (Rolfston)
Species: Vampire
Mate: Shaye
Job: Investments, day trading, Clan leader
Special Abilities: Telepathy, shielding
Book: Bite Me Again

Shaye
Species: Human/Vampire
Mate: Rolf
Job: Nurse
Special Abilities: Healing
Book: Bite Me Again

Sam

Species: Werewolf
Mate: Tess
Job: Brewer/Chef/Owner, Black Wolf Brewery
Rolf's friend
Book: A Hairy Situation

Tess

Species: Witch
Mate: Sam
Job: Medical coder, nurse
Shaye's friend
Book: A Hairy Situation

Emma (Emmaline)

Species: Vampire
Mate: Doc (Albert)
Job: Landowner/small farm
Special Abilities: Visions/Premonitions
Rolfston's mother
Book: Pointed Love

Doc (Dr. T, Albert)

Species: Alicorn
Mate: Emma
Job: Doctor
*Special Abilities: Some healing, visions, magic,
    immortality*
Book: Pointed Love

Ian
Species: Vampire
Mate: Berkley
Job: Leathersmith, Blacksmith
Special Abilities: Speed
Shaye's friend
Book: Forged In Love

Berkley
Species: Fae
Mate: Ian
Job: Owner/Potter, The Winged Potter
*Special Abilities: Can sense auras and species, slight
    healing ability, senses magic/spells*
Rolf's friend
Book: Forged In Love

Gawain
Species: Falcon shifter
Mate: Merri
Job: Historian/archeologist
Rolf's friend
Book: Linked in History

Merri (Meredith)
Species: Witch
Mate: Gawain
Job: Librarian
Tess's sister
Book: Linked in History

Vlad (Vladimir)

Species: Vampire

Evil father of Rolfston

Note: Appeared in Bite Me Again. *Vlad had been attempting to gain supporters to take over the paranormal world. When Rolf wouldn't join him, he tried to kill him.*

Sheriff (Gage)

Species: Griffin

Mate: none (yet)

Job: Sheriff of Rockfort, Warden

Special Abilities: Very strong magic, tracking magic, can tell other rare paranormals

Duncan

Species: Dragon

Mate: Marge

Job: Sculptor

Special Abilities: Dragon fire

Note: Vlad killed his sister. Assisted in battle in Bite Me Again.

Book: Hoarded Secrets

Marge

Species: Cat shifter, black jaguar

Mate: Duncan

Job: Librarian in Rockfort, Guardian of the Library

Book: Hoarded Secrets

Marco

Species: Gargoyle
Job: Hunter for Wardens
Special Abilities: Tracking
Note: Warden, Gage's brother. Helps the Clan in A
Hairy Situation, Forged In Love, Linked In
History.

Jimmy

Species: Otter
Special Abilities: TruthSpeaker
*Note: Kidnapped by Barry, helped Marge. Adopted
by Marge and Duncan.*
Book: Hoarded Secrets

MINOR CHARACTERS

Samantha

Species: Brownie
*Note: Caretaker for Emma's farm in England,
weaves, and quilts blankets. Mentioned in*
Pointed Love.

Douglas

Species: Gnome
Note: Ferrier, Sculptor, helps on Emma's farm.
Mentioned in Pointed Love.

Thalia

Species: Unicorn
Note: Doc's mentor growing up, deceased.
Mentioned in Pointed Love. *Healer.*

Jacob

Species: Human
Mate: Terrance (bear)
Note: Emma's friend, deceased. Mentioned in Pointed Love. *Nickname Hennie Pie. Emma's farmhand when she was human in England.*

Ter (Terrance)

Species: Bear shifter
Mate: Jacob
Note: Deceased. Mated to Emma's friend Jacob (mated in the afterlife). Mentioned in Pointed Love.

Charlotte

Species: Human/Vampire
Note: Ian's mom. Mentioned in Forged In Love. *Farmer.*

James

Species: Human/Vampire
Note: Ian's dad, Mentioned in Forged In Love. *Farmer, blacksmith.*

Robert

Species: Vampire
Mate: Aggie (Ian's aunt)
Special Abilities: Speed
Note: Ian's uncle in-law. Mentioned in Forged In Love. *A Lord (in England).*

Agnes (Aggie)

Species: Human/Vampire
Mate: Robert
Note: Ian's aunt. Mentioned in Forged In Love.
Artist (painter)

George

Species: Vampire
Mate: Matthew
Book: Mentioned in Forged in Love. *Note: Robert's brother. Robert is Ian's uncle.*

Matthew

Species: Vampire
Mate: George
Book: Mentioned in Forged in Love.

Clara

Species: Vampire
Book: Mentioned in Forged In Love. *Ian's cousin. Currently a Broadway actor.*

George

Species: Human
Book: Mentioned in A Hairy Situation, *Sam's produce supplier.*

Graeme

Species: Human
Book: Mentioned in Forged In Love, *showed Ian around his workshop, discussed ideas for Ian's own forge. Blacksmith.*

Bert
Species: Human
Book: Mentioned in Forged In Love, *part of the hunter group that shot Ian.*

Carly
Species: Human
Book: Mentioned in Forged In Love, *young nosy cashier in Ian's parents' town.*

Dan
Species: Vampire
Book: Mentioned in Bite Me Again, A Hairy Situation, *Vlad minion. Attacked Sam/Tess.*

Roger
Species: Vampire
Book: Mentioned in Bite Me Again, A Hairy Situation, *Vlad minion. Attacked Sam/Tess. Delivered poisoned blood to clinic/Rolf in* Bite Me Again.

Tim
Species: Human
Book: Mentioned in Pointed Love. *Wood carver at winter market. Shelly (wife), Natalie (daughter, just had baby girl), 2 sons.*

Rob
Species: Unknown/Paranormal
Book: Mentioned in Linked In History. *Archeologist, friend of Gawain.*

Daryl
Species: Jackalope

Book: Mentioned in Linked In History. *Rob's dig was on his land.*

Barry
Species: Vampire
Book: Mentioned in Linked In History. *Convocation member.*

Randy
Species: Alligator
Book: Mentioned in Linked In History. *Archeologist.*

Rick
Species: Human
Book: Mentioned in Linked In History. *Sheriff near Yellowstone, friend of Gage. Human but has paranormals in his family.*

Rhonda
Species: Bear shifter
Book: Mentioned in Linked In History. *Shopkeeper in town.*

Angie
Species: Human
Book: Mentioned in Linked In History. *Hotel front desk.*

Steve
Species: Human
Book: Mentioned in Hoarded Secrets. *Disbelieving townsperson.*
Mate: Marshall

Marshall
Species: Tortoise, mechanic in Rockfort
Book: Mentioned in Hoarded Secrets
Mate: Steve

Paul
Species: Human
Book: Mentioned in Hoarded Secrets. *Almost hit Marshall as a turtle. Has pet rabbit.*

Gary
Species: Unknown
Book: Mentioned in Hoarded Secrets. *Lawn care, handyman.*

Dave Youger
Species: Witch
Book: Mentioned in Hoarded Secrets. *Friend of Jimmy.*

Sherri
Species: Human
Job: Receptionist at Doc's clinic

Beth
Species: Human
Mate: Josh (witch)
Job: Florist/Owner, Rockfort Blooms.

Mary
Species: Human
Mate: Bill
Job: Bakery owner

Bill
Species: Human
Mate: Mary
Job: Bakery owner

Marge's library apartment
(pre renovations)

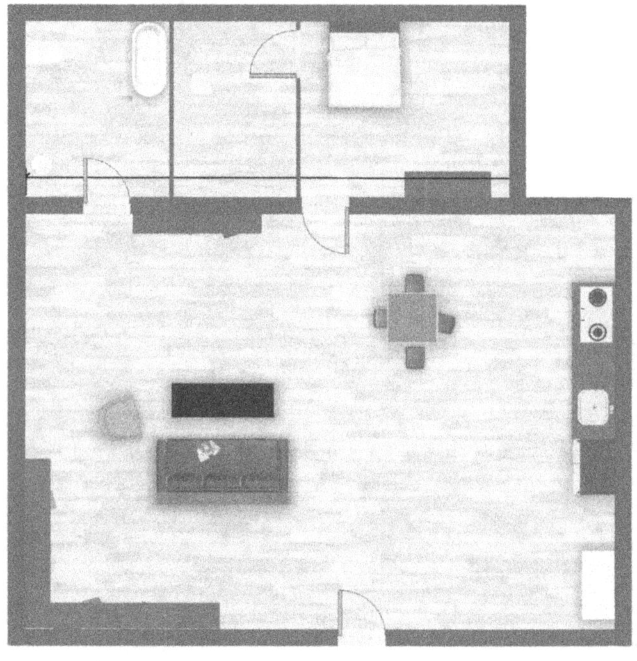

Marge's library apartment
(post renovations)

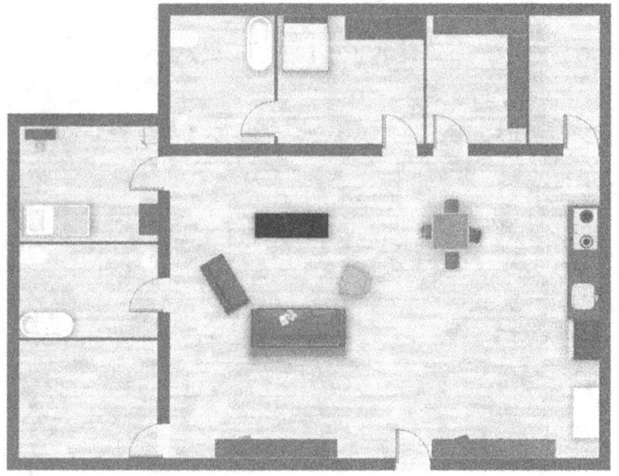

Paranormal History Museum 1st Floor

Paranormal History Museum 2nd Floor

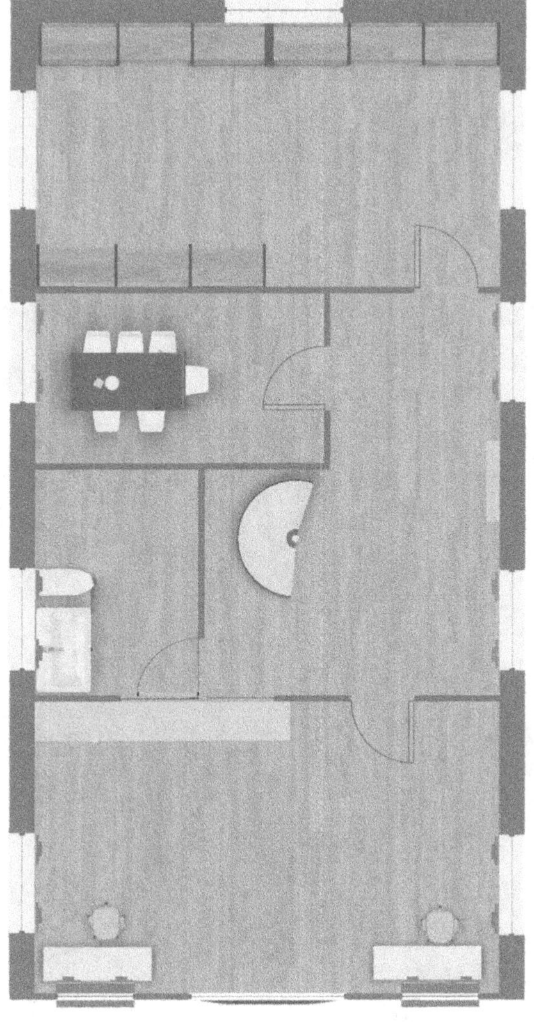

ABOUT THE AUTHOR

I have loved reading since I was a child. I also enjoy baking, photography, and seeing new things. My favorite books are romances with a happily ever after. The world is a crazy place; sometimes escaping into a great book is the only way I can truly relax. Happily ever after is my favorite type of book, so my stories will end with a HEA, even if the road is a little bumpy getting there. I currently reside in the Midwest with my family.

If you sign up for my newsletter, you will get a free short story! *Christmas with the Nightwood Clan* is a glimpse into the Clan's first Christmas together and takes place during the Christmas in *A Hairy Situation*.

www.HarperDakota.com
www.Harper Dakota.com/newsletter
Harper's Readers Group

ALSO BY THE AUTHOR

Bite Me Again (Nightwood Clan, 1)

A Hairy Situation (Nightwood Clan, 2)

Pointed Love (Nightwood Clan, 3)

Forged In Love (Nightwood Clan, 4)

Linked In History (Nightwood Clan, 5)

Hoarded Secrets (Nightwood Clan, 6)

Warded Bonds (Coming Soon. Nightwood Clan, 7)

The Nightwood Clan's Favorite Recipes